G Stands for Gun

**Center Point
Large Print**

**This Large Print Book carries the
Seal of Approval of N.A.V.H.**

NELSON NYE

G Stands for Gun

CENTER POINT PUBLISHING
THORNDIKE, MAINE

This Center Point Large Print edition
is published in the year 2004 by arrangement with
Golden West Literary Agency.

The text of this Large Print edition is unabridged. In other
aspects, this book may vary from the original edition. Printed in
Thailand. Set in 16-point Times New Roman type by
Bill Coskrey and Gary Socquet.

ISBN 1-58547-401-0

Library of Congress Cataloging-in-Publication Data

Nye, Nelson C. (Nelson Coral), 1907-
    G stands for gun / Nelson C. Nye.--Center Point large print ed.
      p. cm.
    ISBN 1-58547-401-0 (lib. bdg. : alk. paper)
      1. Large type books. I. Title.

PS3527.Y33G 2004
813'.54--dc22

2003021319

CHAPTER ONE

BEHIND the counter of the Come-An'-Get-It restaurant, the red-haired girl abruptly stemmed the crimson tide of her invective. Curiosity merged with the dark blue wrath in her stormy eyes as she swept an appraising glance across the lean figure of the man standing solidly just inside the swinging door.

Strangers, to Lisabet Corbin's experience, were common as rubble-rock in Tortilla Flat since the discovery of gold and copper deposits in the Superstitions two months back had boomed the town. But a *gentleman* was a thing uncommon rare.

Hoisting herself to a comfortable perch upon the back counter, Lisabet Corbin suspended her detailed libel of Stone Latham's ancestry, let the gum lay idle in her mouth while gravely she studied the sample Fate had sent her.

The unknown was broad of shoulder, wiry-waisted and lean of hip; a dusty, leather-faced man in worn range garb. Discovery of a stubborn chin, a hawk's beak nose and determined lips, that just now were curved in a faint smile, rewarded her scrutiny. But it was his eyes that caught her instant interest. They were gray, like smoky sage, and serene and confident and quiet as they rested on Stone Latham's darkly scowling face.

Stone Latham's lips twisted in a sneer and his lantern jaw swung belligerently forward. "What was that crack?" he said.

The four late customers ranging the stools along the plank counter stared at the stranger with an air of expectancy which told of their knowledge of Latham's prowess.

"I said," the stranger drawled, still faintly smiling, "that a man-sized gent had ought to be able to find better ways of amusin' himself than baitin' a defenceless girl."

Stone Latham, as the watchers caught their breaths in a united "Ah!" swept the stranger with a slow insolent glance that passed from head to feet.

"Are you aimin' to make somethin' out of it, pilgrim?"

The stranger's grin disclosed twin sets of hard white teeth. "Shucks," he said, "I was just makin' a observation, so to speak."

"Yeah? Well, observations is dangerous as hell in this man's town. I'd admire to hear y'u take that 'un back right pronto!"

The stranger made no reply. He stood there easily, his hands hanging at his sides, the lazy smile still on his lips. Then suddenly he laughed.

Lisabet Corbin tingled to a swift cold thrill as Stone Latham, his right hand dropping to his holstered gun, took three long steps toward the mocking stranger and flung back his left hand, palm open, to slap the stranger's face.

It was an old affair, this trick of Latham's. It was a thing Lisabet Corbin had seen Latham get away with time after time. For, timed to the sound of his slap, his naked right-hand gun had always either intimidated his

6

victim or brought him to a speedy grave.

It was intended to do so now. With his right hand clamped about gun-butt, Stone Latham's left hand started toward the stranger's face.

But this time Latham's blow was not permitted to land. He checked it in mid-air. And for the most excellent of reasons—something cold and hard and rigid was pressed uncomfortably against his stomach.

The stranger's grin grew wider, but there was nothing humorous in the gray depths of his cold-eyed glance as he drawled:

"You're keepin' the lady waitin', hombre. She an' me is cravin' to hear you orate as how them disrespectful words of yourn was lies. An' you better orate quick."

An angry red washed into Stone Latham's scowling cheeks, then, swiftly fading, left them a sickly sallow gray. For the space of a hasty heartbeat he hesitated, then his hand came away from his gun and joined its mate above his head.

"I reckon," he growled thickly, "I was thinkin' about some oth—about someone else."

The something cold and hard and rigid dug deeper into the flabby muscles of Latham's stomach. "An' I expect you're allowin'," the stranger's drawl was inexorable, "that this lady's reputation is plumb unreproachable, that there was no occasion for either your remark or the insinuatin' sneer on your kisser, an' that in the future you'll see that it goes hard with any polecat that maligns her in your hearin'?"

Stone Latham licked burning lips while a vein throbbed wildly on his temple. His eyes were ven-

7

omous with hate when he finally snarled:

"That—that's right."

The stranger stepped back with an easy smile, exposing the fact that he'd menaced Latham with nothing more dangerous than a rigid index finger.

But though the watchers saw, none snickered.

Stone Latham, when he could trust his voice, said wickedly, "I'll be rememb'rin' that. An' I'll be rememb'rin' *you!*"

The stranger's smoky eyes grew mocking.

"Shucks," he smiled, "I'd feel cheated if you didn't."

Latham shoved the swinging door wide and strode angrily forth into the dusty night, followed a moment later by two of the stool-warmers. The two remaining customers, as the stranger moved forward, withdrew to the counter's far end and opened a low-voiced, well-gestured conversation.

"Concernin' me," the stranger told himself. Aloud he said to the girl, "I'll have some ham, an' aiggs, ma'am, an' a cup of black java."

She leaned toward him across the counter and her eyes, twin pools of slumbering passion, were deep and dark and blue. "Y'u hadn't ought to have took up for me, stranger. Stone Latham's a bad man to cross. He's orn'ry enough to carry sheep dip an' he'll lay for y'u sure."

"I don't expect I'll be worryin' a heap about Mr. Latham," the stranger shrugged. "I reckon his bark's a lot meaner'n his bite."

"Y'u don't know Stone Latham," the girl said

earnestly. "I'm wantin' to thank y'u for what y'u done for me, an' I'm wantin' to give y'u a piece of good advice. Get on yore hoss an' get out of these mountains quick."

"Shucks, I couldn't do that noways, ma'am. I'm figurin' to bed down here an' stay a spell. I allow I'm goin' to like this town."

"This town," she said vehemently, "is a place where a sidewinder would be ashamed to see his mother!"

"Shucks," the stranger chuckled. "I reckon it ain't that bad. Why, you're here, ma'am."

Her red lips twisted. "I fit the town, Mister, as y'u'll learn quick if y'u insist on stayin' here till someone plants y'u. 'Cordin' to the lights of *decent* people, Stone Latham jest told Lize Corbin to her face what they've been sayin' behind her back for weeks."

Her blue eyes probed the smoky gray ones of the stranger as she defiantly added, "I'm Lisabet Corbin. Folks here call me Lize—when they ain't callin' me somethin' worse."

The stranger doffed his shabby hat and smiled infectiously. "Why, ma'am, I'm proud to know you. I'm S. G. Shane, though mostly I'm knowed as 'Sudden.' I reckon you an' me will get along first rate."

An instant longer her probing stare remained upon his face. Then abruptly she turned away. But not before he'd seen a telltale sign of moisture in her eyes. He shook his head a little grimly. Poor kid! Evidently she had lost what some people valued above all else—her reputation. Probably some man had made a fool of her, had somehow taken advantage of her, and this hairy-chested Tortilla Flat had rubbed salt in her wounds. Towns were like that, he mused; once a woman strayed from the straight and narrow they could not rest till they'd dragged her down and clogged her path with mire.

He studied her as she moved about the stove, stirring up a batch of tantalizing aromas as she worked preparing his meal. Her hair, so flaming red, was alive with glinty gleams of copper where the lamplight struck across it, and was openly rebellious as though never having known the curbing influence of comb or brush. Hers was a vital figure, alive with life and natural grace. She was like some wild thing held captive in a cage. Belted overalls and a blue flannel shirt such as riders wear detracted nothing from her primal loveliness; the faded jeans but emphasized the slender longness of her shapely legs, and her flannel shirt but accentuated the alluring contour of her breasts. He admired her clean-limbed stride and the pluck that would not let her run away, but held her here to face the slurs and slander of this gold camp.

She placed the meal before him. "Y'u came from Texas, didn't y'u?"

Her unexpected question drew a frown. But the frown swiftly faded beneath a grin. "I reckon you called the turn, ma'am. You didn't see my hoss by any chance?"

"Y'u got the look of a Texas man," she said, adding, "I'm from Texas, too—way back. My Dad was a West Texas cattle man. My mother died when I was a kid. Then Dad he got the gold fever an' we been followin' the gold camps ever since."

"An' where's your Dad now, if I might ask?"

"If y'u was to ask folks back round Pecos, an' they'd heard the news, I reckon they'd opine he was in heaven," she said slowly, wistfully. "But if y'u was to put that question to the mavericks of Tortilla Flat they'd tell y'u Dry-Camp Corbin—the ol' fool—was down in hell wheah he belonged. Y'u see, one of Jarson Lume's gun-slicks downed him when a rumor got spreadin' round he'd struck it rich."

Shane sat up straighter on his stool. His face seemed whiter and his chin thrust forward grimly.

"Jarson Lume, eh?" his voice was cold with a crackly crispness that drew the attention of the two stool-warmers at the counter's farther end. "I've heard that name before, ma'am. He's some pumpkins round these diggin's, I reckon?"

"He's top screw," said a cold, grim voice from the doorway. "An' he's some partic'lar who tosses his name around."

Mr. Sudden Shane paid no attention to the interruption; he did not even turn his head to examine the speaker. His eyes remained on the girl's face, taking note of the sudden color that stained her cheeks and the look of mingled anger, loathing and resentment which, at the sound of the newcomer's voice, had flashed into her stormy eyes.

"You was sayin', ma'am?" Shane queried.

But Lisabet Corbin was not listening. Her blazing eyes were fixed above and beyond his shoulder; on the man at the door, he guessed. With one swift lunge her right hand dropped beneath the counter and came up

11

with a sawed-off shotgun.

"Get outa here, y'u polecat!"

A harsh laugh a-drip with insolent mockery struck the ears of Sudden Shane. He turned, then, slowly on his stool and let his calm, appraising glance play over the newcomer.

The man by the door had a cold, bloodless face, handsome despite the tight, thin-lipped mouth and foppish tiny black mustache. He was clad in the flat-rimmed hat, frock coat and black string tie of the professional gambler. He fingered his tiny mustache with a characteristic gesture and laughed again, slowly, softly, now.

"My dear, you are letting your nerves get the best of you. When I entered I believe I heard you and this, ah— gentleman—discussing me. Haven't you learned that it's bad form discussing a man behind his back? Tut, tut, my dear, tut, tut! Give you time and you'll learn a lot, I'm sure."

Deliberately ignoring both the girl and her shaking weapon, the man in gambler's clothes now turned to Shane. "I don't believe I have the pleasure of your acquaintance, sir."

"If you think it'll be a pleasure, you're mistaken," Shane drawled coldly. "I've got no use for woman-baitin' skunks."

No expression on the gambler's immobile countenance betrayed his feelings. No least twitching muscle gave any fraction of his thoughts away. His unwinking flinty eyes were baffling as he said,

"Neither have I. I'm Jarson Lume, stranger. I own the Square Deal, a gentleman's resort across the street. I don't believe I caught your name?"

"I don't expect you did."

"Hmm. I understand you had a little run-in with Stone Latham a few minutes ago. I know Latham pretty well and I'd like to warn you that he's not a forgiving man."

"I'm powerful astonished to find we've somethin' in common," Shane commented, and turned back to his meal. The girl was no longer in evidence and he guessed she had retired to the back room to escape Lume's obviously unwelcome company.

Lume came up and took a stool beside Shane. He gave the two men at the other end of the counter a long silent scrutiny at which, dropping coins to pay for their grub, they got up and slunk away.

"Got 'em pretty well gentled, ain't you?" Shane commented.

"Look here, stranger; it strikes me you're adoptin' the wrong attitude here—" Lume began, when Shane cut in curtly:

"My attitude suits me right down to the ground."

"Well, it don't suit me, by Gawd, an' what I say in this town goes!" Lume growled. "There ain't no middle course in Tortilla Flat; folks that ain't for me are against me—an' fools who are against me have a habit of kickin' off sudden. Do I make myself clear?"

Shane grinned. "What you got in mind?"

For a moment Lume eyed him intently, then relaxed. "That's better. You're showin' good sense. From what I heard about your run-in with Latham, you've got guts. I've got plenty of jobs for men of your caliber," he added, and paused suggestively.

"I ain't exactly in need of work," Shane said slowly. "Got a bit of cash left over from my last . . . job. But I'm always willin' to lend a open ear to a good proposition. What you got in mind?"

A faint smile fleetingly crossed the gambler's thin lips, but he took care not to let Shane see it. "Well, I'll tell you," he said confidentially. "I need a man to take a shipment of gold out to Phoenix. 'Course the stage'll take it out, you understand. But I need a gent on the box that'll see my shipment goes through without a hitch. I don't dare keep too much money on hand in this camp; too many crooks willin' to risk their necks in a try for it. There's places gettin' stuck up here right and left. Had three robberies in town last night. A killing, too."

He looked at Shane keenly, scrutinizing his bronzed countenance as though weighing him, as though striving to determine his potential value. "Yes," he muttered at last, "I've got to get some of my dinero into a bank, an' the sooner the better for all concerned. Trouble is, the stage has been stuck up six times in the last month."

"Kinda wild country up here, I reckon," was Shane's comment. "I can see your angle, though. You want somebody to ride the stage an' see that your shipment ain't taken off."

Jarson Lume nodded. "That's it."

"Got any idea who's pullin' all these stick-ups?"

"I've got notions," Lume admitted, "but nothin' definite enough to act on. This town ain't got its growth an' she's tough as hell. A man has to be right careful what he says around here unless he's got a hankering for

14

Boot Hill. The way I look at it, it's cheaper to hire a shotgun guard than it is to make accusations without the evidence to back them up.

"There's plenty in this town have got it in for me already. I don't know why, I'm sure. Take Lize Corbin, now," he shot a covert glance at Shane. "She's got some wild notion I had somethin' to do with her old man getting rubbed out. Nothing to it, of course, but there it is. I can't dissuade her of the notion an' she threatens to salivate me every time I set foot on this side of the street.

"Well," he concluded, "do you want the job?"

"Trip to Phoenix an' back, eh? An' after that?"

"More trips. In between times I'll find somethin' else to keep you busy," Lume said easily. "But that comes first. I'll pay you two hundred dollars for the trip—if you get the shipment through."

"Quite generous," Shane commented drily. "An' if I don't?"

"Not one damned cent."

"Fair enough. I reckon you've hired yourself a man. When you shippin'?"

"Stage pulls in from Globe tomorrow afternoon an' leaves for Phoenix tomorrow night at seven sharp. By the way, what am I supposed to call you?"

"Shane—S. G. Shane's the name."

"Glad I met up with you, Shane," Lume said, and held out a lean right hand which Shane somehow failed to grasp. Lume stared hard, endeavoring to make out whether the insult had been deliberate or whether Shane had not noticed his gesture. But he could make nothing of Shane's expression as Shane was looking the other way, toward the door to the rear room in which Lisabet Corbin was angrily pacing the floor. With a curt "So-long," Lume strode softly into the turbulent night.

Shane sat still, and there was an odd little smile on his lips.

CHAPTER TWO

RECKON I misjudged y'u some considerable, Texas Man. I allow y'u are jest about as orn'ry as the rest of the fly-by-night owlhooters that have come driftin' into this here town ever since some damn fool went an' located gold an' copper in Fish Creek Canyon!"

Sudden Shane looked up into the scornful face and contemptuous dark blue eyes of Lisabet Corbin. He did not need a telescope to decipher the anger, the loathing, and the bitter disappointment that filled those flashing orbs. She had weighed him, found him wanting. The heat of a sudden flush warmed his cheeks beneath their bronze.

"Shucks, ma'am," he said, gravely considering her. "Now I reckon you have gone an' jumped to a bad conclusion."

"Damn bad, cowboy—an' I ain't doubtin' it's correct!"

Cold hostility bulged into her voice. "Don't tell me! I saw y'u grinnin' like a chessy cat after yo' palaver with that stinkin' tinhorn!"

"Why, ma'am, I expect you are right about my

16

grinnin', though I hadn't figured I was doin' it that open-like."

"Y'u addle-pated fool! D'y'u think y'u can p'rambulate around with skunks like Lume an' not get to smellin' jest like 'em? If yo' goin' to lay down with dawgs, y'u gotta expect to git up with fleas; I'm a-tellin' y'u!"

"Now, ma'am, I was only——"

"I can't hang that buck in my smoke-house!" she cut him off. "Ain't y'u never heard that jestin' lies brings serious sorrers? I seen y'u an' that—that damn' Lume huddled up gassin'! Thick as cloves on a Christmas ham, y'u was! Shane, I'm rightdown disappointed in y'u!"

"Shucks, ma'am. Don't you reckon I had my reasons?"

"I sure do! Y'u seen which way the wind blowed strongest an' piled yo' hay accordin'. But y'u'll git burnt if y'u go to playin' with Jarson Lume! Him an' Latham an' Bronc Walders an' a bunch more snakes of the same stripe is all mixed up together. Them an' Marshal Wolf Brady—who is a dang coyote—jest about runs this town."

Shane's gray eyes lost their accustomed twinkle and he looked uncomfortably away. She sure was a heap positive in her notions, he reflected. "Shucks, ma'am," he said with a little grin. "You ain't figurin' to class me with them reptiles, are you?"

"Y'u got me fightin' my hat," she admitted angrily. "I jest can't make y'u out! First off, y'u make a monkey outa Latham. Then y'u git thicker'n splatter with

Latham's boss! Y'u got a screw loose someplace? Why, y'u lunkhaid, them scorpions'll jest natcherly tie y'u up in knots! But go ahead—I reckon y'u been weaned some time. If y'u wanta hitch up with them varmints it's yo' business an' none of mine.

"But I'm a-tellin' y'u," her red lips hardened in a bitter line and her voice came thickly, as though choked with feeling, "if yo' goin' to run with them y'u can't eat here. That's final! Slap yo' dinero on the counter an' git goin'."

"But ma'am!" Shane expostulated "This Lume jasper offered me a job! Ain't nothin' wrong in takin' a job— even with a tarantula—is there?"

"Job, hell! Don't y'u know that butcher-bird's jest fixin' to git y'u killed off nice an' safe? I bet he offered y'u a job ridin' shotgun to a shipment of dust an' nuggets! Didn't he?"

The cold contempt in her flashing eyes had not abated by a fraction. Shane stirred uneasily under her fixed regard. "Well," he admitted reluctantly, "he did offer—"

"I knew it!" she snapped vindictively. "Why, y'u dang lunkhaid! D'y'u think that slick coyote ain't got y'u figgered plumb center? Yo' the fifth fool he's hired fo' that job!"

"The fifth? What's happened to the others?" Shane asked innocently.

"Three of 'em got killed tryin' to scare off stick-ups an' the other one—'cordin' to Jarson Lume's tellin'— tried to skip off with the shipment himself. The driver," she paused to glower at him scathingly, "blowed his brains out!"

Shane's glance searched her face intently. "Are you runnin' on me, ma'am?"

"Do I look like the runnin' kind?"

"Well, but that's terrible, ma'am."

"I allow that's what them four guards thought when they was cashin' in their chips! Y'u can't play round with Jarson Lume."

"But, ma'am, he wouldn't dare pull nothin' so raw as that—" Shane began, when her short laugh cut him off.

"Listen," she told him. "Jarson Lume would dare anythin' if he saw sufficient profit. I'm a-tellin' y'u. I know that polecat from hocks to horns!"

"But mebbe—"

"There ain't no buts to it, Texas Man. If y'u are Lume-minded, y'u'll play yo' hand out as y'u see fit. Y'u sort of throwed in to do me a good turn tonight so I'm a-warnin' y'u. I don't aim to be beholdin' to no damn man. I've passed y'u the word; y'u can take it or leave it. It's up to y'u. Now clear outa here; I'm figurin' to close up pronto."

From open doors and windows great splotches of golden light seeped out across the hock-deep dust of Tortilla Flat's single crooked street, collecting in pools that but accentuated the sullen darkness of the moonless night.

Oil flares, placed at appropriate intervals, served to illuminate the misspelled legends scrawled across the high false fronts of the town's flimsy buildings, and painted on the garish signs hung out above the town's plank sidewalks.

There were saloons and gambling halls, a hotel, several blacksmith shops, two stores and three honkytonks. The largest honkytonk was Gar-Faced Nell's Place—a brothel of the lowest type. Everything went inside its tarpaper walls, and many a gent had its denizens seen rolled and chucked out in the dusty street to sleep off his knockout drops.

But the biggest resort of all, a combination dance hall, gambling hell and saloon, was the Square Deal—owned and operated by the poker-faced Jarson Lume.

Tortilla Flat's main stem was not a long one, but it fairly teemed with life. Cowpunchers rubbed elbows with hairy-faced and red-shirted miners; sleek, pale steerers walked cheek by jowl with mining engineers and cattle magnates; tinhorns, barkers, come-ons, homesteaders and pimps—all mingled freely in the flotsam-jetsam composing the boom-town's boisterous population. Many of the big, burly fellows one could see on every hand walked with the rolling gait of the dismounted horseman. More than an equal number were horny-handed from grubbing in the soil and cliffs and creeks of the surrounding mountains.

When Sudden Shane stepped out upon the planks before the Lone Star Grub Emporium there was a tiny smile on his genial lips. A twinkle came into his eyes as he recalled the girl's warning. Lize Corbin was a good sort, he reflected; undoubtedly tomboyish, yet every inch a man's woman from her flaming head to her booted feet. Grace was in her every movement; she was possessed of a pantherish vitality and had a tremendous store of nervous energy and pluck. Not many women, he told himself, would have the nerve to outface this hell-roaring camp and tell it in plain terms what she thought of it and the men who bossed it. There was, he felt, much about her for a discerning man to admire. In the parlance of the country she was a "square-shooter"—he would cheerfully have bet his last dollar on the fact had he been called upon to do so.

And someone in this coyote town, some two-legged varmint calling itself a man, had handed her a raw deal lately. He would have known it even had he not over-heard Stone Latham's slurring remark. The fact was patent in the defiant tilt of her chin and in the resentful light of her stormy eyes. These bespoke, to Shane's mind, the decent woman putting up a plucky front to a sneering world. He was all for her; but he did not intend to let her influence his plans or sway him from the course of action he had determined to adopt.

With the thought his jaw swung forward stubbornly; nothing should prevent him from accomplishing his aim, or sidetrack him from the purpose which had brought him here.

Mounting his horse he urged the animal down the dusty road till he reached the Miner's Rest, and there tied his mount to the scarred hitching rail among a group of others. With saddlebags across his shoulder he mounted the board steps and strode into the dingy office.

Several men were seated in its restricted space with chairs tilted comfortably back against the walls. None of these displayed the least interest in Shane until he said:

"I'd be obliged for a room. Be wantin' it indefinitely. How much?"

A bald-headed man with beetling brows looked up at him, arching his shaggy brows inquiringly. "Stranger, ain't y'u?"

Shane looked thoughtful while the others eyed him curiously. He pushed his hat back to scratch his head; brushed the corn-colored shock of hair back off his forehead and suddenly grinned. "Well, yes," he finally admitted. "I reckon I could be fitted into that category. Ah—how about that room?"

The beetling-browed man stared at the others; they stared back. One of them, a tall man with heavy face and long, drooping mustache, nodded slightly.

The bald-headed man cleared his throat. "I can let you have a room, stranger. But she'll cost y'u right smart. My rooms rent for ten bucks a day."

Shane grinned. "I didn't aim to buy it," he said.

"Y'u couldn't buy it fer all the gold in this camp, stranger. Rooms is scarce in Tortilla. I've charged—"

"Listen, fella. If I had ten bucks I wouldn't be wantin' your room."

"Huh?"

"I wouldn't be wantin' it because I'd be afraid for my life in here with that much dinero on me."

"Are y'u tryin' to be funny, mister?" the bald-headed man demanded with a scowl. "Ten bucks a room is my price—an' it's payable in advance."

"Well," Shane said, turning toward the door, "I sure hope you'll be able to rent it."

"Hey—where y'u goin'?"

22

"I'm goin' to fix me up a deal with one of these resort-owners," Shane said, and went on out.

He climbed into the saddle and rode back along the dusty road till he reached the Square Deal. There he dismounted and, tying his buckskin, entered the resort.

When his eyes had grown accustomed to the glare of the coal-oil lamps that were bracketed about the great barn-like room, he leveled a quick glance through the wavering haze of tobacco smoke. But he did not immediately see Jarson Lume.

Making his way to the long plank bar he joined the line of men bellying it and had a drink. It was while he was toying with his second, that he saw the coldly handsome face of the Square Deal's frock-coated owner.

Lume saw him at the same time and came toward him, stopping momentarily a number of times to return the greetings of acquaintances. When Lume came up he reached out a lean white hand. "Glad to see you here, Shane. Havin' a good time?"

Shane shook his hand with a show of cordiality. "I allow I'm gettin' around. Can you tell me where I can find a place to put up?"

"Well," said Lume, "there's the Miner's Rest down the street. They might take you or I could put you up here, if you don't mind doubling up with one of the boys."

"Mebbe I'd better put up here, where I can be handy in case you want me for anythin'."

"Good idea. Go up the stairs over there an' go along the balcony till you locate room number ten. If there's

23

anyone in it'll be Bill Halleck. He runs one of the faro layouts here. He's off tonight. 'F he happens to be up there, just tell him I said you were to put up with him."

Shane nodded and started for the stairs. As he skirted the dance floor the music being furnished by the sage-brush orchestra came to a stop. Followed a stamping of feet and clink of spurs interspersed with the tapping of high-heeled slippers as couples started off the floor. A number of near-tight customers bumped into Shane who passed the encounters off with grins. He had almost reached the stairs when he came face to face with Stone Latham, a frowsy, scantily-clad blonde clinging to his arm.

Stone Latham came to a jolting stop, a bold intentness in his glance, a cynical curve to his lips. There were men who had hinted that Latham's folks on his mother's side had worn moccasins, that he would rather take his man in the back than elsewhere and was partial to a knife, but Shane could tell by a look at his heavy eyes that such hints had not been made in Latham's presence. For though the man had swagger, there was something about him that told Shane he'd plenty of nerve to back his swagger up.

Latham said, "Still here an' on top the ground, eh?" and his dark, lean-carved face crinkled into a grin, a grin, however, that was not matched by the light in his eyes.

Out of the corner of his eye, Shane saw Jarson Lume coming toward them. He flashed his teeth at Latham and was about to pass on to the stairs, but Latham's left hand reached out and caught his arm.

"Just a minute, fella. I got some good advice for you. Pull your picket pin an' drift before a hunk of lead cuts sho't your rope."

"Is that a warnin'?"

"Just good advice; you better heed it." Relinquishing Shane's arm, Latham moved off with his blonde enchantress.

Shane grimaced and went up the stairs. He quickly found the door with a crayoned #10 upon it, but stopped irresolute as his hand reached out for the knob. The sound of voices came from beyond the door; a girlish giggle, a half-hearted protest and a man's deep growl.

Shane's lips tightened. "I'm thinkin' Bill Halleck won't be wantin' to be disturbed just now," he told himself, and retraced his way down the stairs. Reaching the bottom he took out his watch and squinted an eye at its dial. Ten after twelve. Much too early to turn in, in an all-night town. "Mebbe I better go out a spell an' mosey around takin' in the sights," he mused, and made his way to the door.

He stepped outside, saw a man fumbling with his pony's reins.

"Get your hands off that hoss!" he snapped, and started forward.

As he cleared the porch something tugged at his open vest and a shot rang out, slamming against the buildings across the street. Shane stopped short and a second slug ripped through his hat. He caught the flash this time and his gun came out and up, bucked viciously against his palm as a livid flame belched outward from its muzzle. Came a blur of movement from the man beside his horse, but the fellow wasn't fast enough. Shane's shot struck him in the chest and smashed him backward out of sight.

He whirled in time to see the first man sprinting desperately toward a building corner, men ducking from his path as though from a plague. With a shake of the head Shane let him go. He was returning his gun to leather when a heavy hand fell on his shoulder and whirled him round. A tall man faced him and he felt the man's gun shoved into his stomach—hard.

The man's face was tautly parted over the yellowed teeth behind his drooping black mustache. His voice had a leaping rasp, "Hell's lookin' you in the eye, stranger—one move an' you're due for plantin'!"

CHAPTER THREE

SHANE read murder in the tall man's heavy face, and for a long-drawn moment remained utterly motionless while silence spread a sound-proof blanket across the roaring camp. No faintest whisper disturbed the breathless hush.

Almost curiously, one might have said, he searched the tall man's face, noting the long, drooping mustache, the brown hair and the piercing black eyes beneath the shaggy, scowling brows. He remembered; this was the man he had seen in the Miner's Rest—the fellow toward whom the others had looked for orders.

Shane's seeking glance rested fleetingly upon the tense whiteness of this man's fingers where they gripped the prodding gun. A shiver, it almost seemed, would have caused that gun to roar.

Then a hard grin cut Shane's bronzed jowls angularly.

"Why, you look some peeved," he said.

An oath fell softly from the tall man's lips. "I'm waitin' to hear whyfor you cut down on Groll that way."

Shane looked to where the boots of the man he'd gunned showed grotesque and motionless in a cleared patch between the horse's hoofs. "I allow," he drawled, "you're referrin' to the fella that was figurin' to make off with my hoss. Where I come from, the little fittin' reward for a hoss thief is a hasty chunk of Mr. Colt's fodder. Are you hintin' it's a crime to kill a hoss thief?"

"We're partic'lar who does the killin' in this man's town. By Gawd, I've got a notion to git up a string party in yore honor!"

Shane's serene gray eyes met the other's calmly. "You represent the entertainment committee?"

"I represent the law, by Gawd!" the tall man's tawny eyes seemed sheathed in a scarlet fog, his twisted lips wreathed a malignant snarl. "Who do you think you are?"

"Me?" Shane seemed surprised. "I'm S. G. Shane."

"Yeah? Well, here's some damn good advice for you, Mister S. G. Shane: This here's a peaceful camp what ain't none partial to killers an' such like. 'F you figure to keep head an' body together, by Gawd, you better git outa this town 'fore daylight. It's the Law talkin' at you—Me, Marshal Wolf Brady!"

"That so?"

"You're damn-well right it's so! All the signs is pointin'—"

27

"I never did believe a heap in signs," Shane's cool drawl cut in.

"You better believe in these signs, Mister; they're pointin' to a quick grave, an' the hole is jest yore size! Git out before daylight or you'll be planted here permanent!"

The collected crowd broke slowly up and disintegrated as, without another word, Marshal Brady wheeled and strode away.

Shane's low chuckle was rich with music. He did not appear greatly worried, and wasn't. "Shucks," he told himself, "it looks like I'm goin' to be right unpopular 'round Tortilla Flat."

Having extracted the spent shells from his gun and reloaded the emptied chambers, he sheathed it and strolled leisurely down the plank sidewalk, studying the heterogeneous mass of humanity which surged unendingly up and down the dusty street.

Here a three-card-monte man plied his doubtful trade upon a tiny three-legged table. There a shell-game artist operated. Over yonder a man barked loudly of the theoretical value of some pet mining stock. He discouraged a sallow-faced, shifty-eyed advertiser of a house of joy and sauntered on. It was an interesting town, he could see; a place of turbulence where life must hang upon the swiftness of a man's trigger-finger.

As he reached the intersection of an alley angling away between a pair of crazily-leaning buildings, a woman's scream stopped him. Thinly it knifed through the scraping fiddles and stamping feet, through the heavy murmurous drone that was the voice of this Tortilla Flat. Tensing, he peered squint-eyed into the drifting shadows between the buildings. Again that scream slid up a sobbing scale that chilled his blood.

Then he was hurtling forward, stumbling through the darkness, his gun gripped ready in his hand.

From out the murk came a strangling sob, the pant of labored breathing, a curse and the slap of struggling bodies. In a window of the building to the right a shade snapped up and flung a bar of yellow light across the alley gloom. A hot, unreasoning anger took Shane as his eyes made out the scene.

In the arms of a lithe, swarthy-faced man struggled a panting, sobbing girl. Even in that instant of snarling wrath Shane realized that her sobs were not born of fear or despair; they were unmistakable sounds of fury.

But he had not paused to analyze these thoughts. As that leaping shade flung its bar of light across the murk he sheathed his gun and sprang. The sound of his striking fist as it met the swarthy chin was like the smack of a board on water. Even as the Mexican's hands fell from about the girl and she pulled free, Shane's left took the man in the stomach and wrung a grunt of agony from his bleeding lips. The swarthy one doubled and Shane's right came up from his boot straps in an uppercut that lifted the would-be seducer clear of the ground and smashed him backward in a sprawling, motionless heap.

Shane's eyes swept to the girl and a startled oath escaped him. It was Lize Corbin and she met his widening stare defiantly as she strove to pull her torn

29

shirt across her jutting breasts.

"Habit of yores, ain't it?"

"You mean rescuing ladies from distress? Why, ma'am, I'm powerful glad I got here when I did," Shane said, and his voice was coldly grim.

It seemed to bring some subtle thrill to the girl for she ceased her movements with the shirt and swayed forward slightly, toward him, some inexplicable light chasing a portion of the storminess from the intent glance that searched his face.

"Y'u ain't mean . . . y'u ain't meanin' that—"

"I'm meanin'," Shane drawled, "that if I'd got here a minute later I'd prob'ly have killed that skunk. An' the Lord knows there's killin's enough chalked up against me now."

The soft light vanished from her eyes and left them bleakly blue. In them swam anger, resentment, a sullen devil-may-care defiance. Yes—and a wistful gleam of disappointment.

But Shane did not see; his eyes and mind were grimly fixed upon that outsprawled figure in the dust. His right hand dropped to gun-butt and his eyes were cold and hard as he waited for the swarthy man to regain consciousness.

The girl touched his arm. "Y'u dished him out plenty, Mister. Leave him be. Tortilla Flat wouldn't call what he was fixin' to do no killin' crime." Her ripe red lips twisted bitterly. "He was only aimin' to spark Lize Corbin, an' the whole town knows she's the property of the first sport that can tame her!"

"I don't like to hear that kinda talk, ma'am. You go

along home, now. What I cal'late to give this two-legged polecat won't be no sight for a woman's eyes to look at."

"Y'u crazy lunkhaid! Ain't y'u in bad enough now with the vinegaronse that run this town—"

Shane cut in, "What handle does this varmint go by?"

"That's Puerco; he's a pal of Marshal Brady. Y'u better leave him be less'n y'u got a hankerin' to be planted 'fore the sun climbs outa bed."

The gleam of Shane's white teeth flashed coldly behind his parted lips. "Shucks, ma'am. Plantin' is a game that two can play."

"Not in this town. The plantin' here is all done by Brady an' Lume an' Latham—'ceptin' for what they hire out to their friends." She seemed, he thought, to want to get him away from here. Probably afraid one of those she'd named might come along. He noticed with a wave of color that in her effort to convince him of her point, she seemed to have forgotten her torn and buttonless shirt. As she leaned forward in her earnestness he could see through a rent in it the rounded contour of a creamy breast. He turned away his eyes in agitation.

"—friends didn't take up where he left off," she was saying passionately, "they'd get theirs back on me after y'u cleared out."

"I don't reckon we need go into that, ma'am. I ain't figurin' to leave. Not yet, leastways. This town has got me interested. The cordial welcome these leadin' citizens been handin' me is rightdown fetchin'. I betcha I'm goin' to be a well known man in Tor—"

"What yo' goin' to be, y'u crazy lunkhaid, is a well-

31

salivated corpse—less'n y'u climb yo' hoss an' burn a trail outen here pronto!"

"Shucks, ma'am, I reckon you're some mistaken." His grin, meant to be assuring, appeared to infuriate her further. She stamped her foot and swore like an angry pirate. "All right, y'u fool!" Wheeling, she turned her back on him and started off. "Don't never say y'u wasn't warned!"

Shane let his glance play over the man he'd felled. A cold, malicious gleam entered his smoky eyes as with a groan the Mexican stirred. The swarthy face writhed painfully. Then the black eyes came blinking open. With a curse the fellow got an elbow under him. Then he saw Shane.

His lambent stare focused sharply, revealing a fiercely malignant blaze of hate as his right hand went streaking hipward toward where the walnut stock of a heavy pistol protruded from an open holster.

Shane drawled softly, "Don't do it, fella. You ain't nearly fast enough."

The swarthy man must have correctly gauged the grim earnestness of that soft drawl, for his reaching hand abruptly stilled. With a grunted oath he got to his feet. "Well?" he glared. "W'at you fixin' to do now, eh?"

"I'm fixin' to give you a piece of good advice. Folks have been givin' me advice ever since I struck this town. Must be catchin' 'cause now I'm givin' you some. Just this, hombre—don't never let me catch you in reachin' distance of Lize Corbin again. That's all. Now *git!*"

The silver of the moonlight and the ochre of these

barren mountains lent a softening languor to a country harsh and spiked by day. But Sudden Shane, as he was known in Texas, gave no attention to the appearance of this land. His glance was alert and keen as he retraced his steps toward the Square Deal, but the brightness of his gaze was not for beauty—it was for a possible hostile move on the part of some hard-case friend of one of these men he had antagonized. He did not mean to be caught napping.

When he reached Jarson Lume's establishment the place was still roaring wide and handsome, though dawn was hardly forty winks away. An all-night place in an all-night town, Shane thought. He grinned tightly for this place was in his blood. A man's town, this, where fortunes hung on the turn of a card or the flip of a knife. A hell-hole, yes—but where life rode swift and high.

He shoved through the Square Deal's swinging doors and got his back against a wall. He stayed there till his eyes grew accustomed to the glare of the coal-oil lamps. Then, peering through the swirling haze of tobacco smoke, he made out the tall, gaunt form of Stone Latham moving toward him with Marshal Brady in his wake.

Shane stood loosely waiting, his arms hanging at his sides.

When the others brought up before him, Shane said, "Latham, you're cuttin' your string pretty short, ain't you?"

His dark and lean-carved face held mockery as Latham answered, "I don't need a long string to handle saddle tramps an' gun-slicks. Don't you reckon you'd better mosey? The Marshal, here, tells me he gave you till daylight to pull your freight. It's gettin' close to daylight now."

"Is it worryin' you?"

"Not me. You're the one that should be doin' the worryin', fella."

Shane laughed coldly. "Well, somehow I don't seem to be. An' I'm allowin' I'll be still in this town long after sun-up, too."

Brady grunted, "That ain't no lie. I've got yore restin' place all picked out—got the coffin measured, too."

"Well, I hope you measured 'er long an' slim, Mister Two-Gun Toter," Shane drawled with a sardonic grin. "Most of the specimens I've seen in this town lean towards a railish figure, an' if anyone occupies your coffin, Brady, the corpse won't look like me."

Latham grinned at the Marshal. "Looks like he's callin' yore hand, Brady. You goin' to let him get away with it?"

Brady sneered. "When the time shoves up, I'll lay him out."

"Yeah?" Shane leaned slightly forward and the smoky gray of his eyes grew darker, dangerous. His tone was low, cold, even:

"This," he said ominously, "is as good a time as any, Brady. I ain't leavin'. What're you goin' to do?"

Brady's bloodshot eyes grew anxious as they studied the tranquil Texan. It was Shane's tranquillity that seemed to bother him most. It was as though he feared Shane had somehow laid a trap for him and now was inviting him to step forward and get himself snared. His hands clenched and unclenched spasmodically while a dull red suffused his cheeks. The Adam's apple bulged in his throat, bounced grotesquely up and down; a barometer indication of the state of his nerves.

Shane's grin was taunting. There was wicked amusement in his eyes as he drawled ironically, "Latham, it looks like the cat run off with your friend's tongue. I'm wantin' to know what he's figurin' to do now that it's settled I'm goin' to remain in this town. Perhaps," his drawl grew softer, "you'd like to take up his burden?"

"Hell," Stone Latham sneered, "I'm not enforcin' the law in this man's town! He's the one that ordered you out. It's up to him to play his hand."

Brady gulped painfully and his eyes slid away from Shane's. "It—it ain't daylight yet," he muttered lamely, and turned away.

Shane looked after him sardonically, and grinned when he noted the redness of the lawman's ears. Then he swung his glance on Latham. "I seem to recall," he said amusedly, "that you, too, was advisin' me to drift last time we met."

Latham's lips curved a cynical smile. "The advice still holds good. But I ain't reckonin' you'll take it. Gunfighters are all alike, to my experience. Each one thinks he can't be beat—till another gent's blue whistler cuts him down."

"D'you think the lead that'll cut me down is in your gun?"

Stone Latham shrugged. *"Quien sabe?"* he said, and walked away.

Shane snorted and climbed the stairs to the balcony. He moved unhurriedly toward the room whose door held a chalk-marked #10. He paused outside a moment. But hearing no sound of voices from within he grasped the knob.

The door was swung on its hinges in such a manner that it opened inward. As Shane turned the knob he gave the door a healthy shove and dropped upon the floor. And lucky that he did!

A jet of flame belched outward from the darkness of the room. Lead sang above his head as his gun was coming out and the smashing report filled the tiny room with reverberating thunder. A wicked smile creased Shane's grim lips as the hammer dropped beneath his thumb. The sound of a falling body reached his ears as booted feet stormed up the balcony stairs.

Swiftly Shane stepped into the room and struck a match. A crumpled figure lay on the floor, a smoking gun still clutched in one outflung hand. Shane studied the narrow face but could not place it as belonging to anyone he knew. "Reckon he's that Bill Halleck jasper I was s'posed to share this two-by-four with," he mused. "Looks like the boss-men of this town are some anxious to get me out of the way. I expect this little trap was Jarson Lume's idea of bein' playful. I wonder how much he knows . . . ?"

The slap of booted feet converging on the room drew him abruptly to his feet. He snuffed the match and dropped it. Sheathing his gun he stepped out onto the balcony and saw half a dozen men sprinting toward him, Brady and Stone Latham in the lead.

At his sudden appearance the running group stopped still.

"Who fired that shot?" Wolf Brady scowled.

"I did, Marshal," Shane drawled evenly. "With my little pistol I fired that shot." His eyes flung a challenge at the staring group. "What you figurin' to do about it?"

"Do! Do?" the marshal spluttered. "Why, dammit, you're under arrest!"

"Take it easy. You'll be gettin' apoplexy if you don't watch out."

With a snarl Wolf Brady's hands flashed hipward and came up in gleaming arcs. But the gun that spoke was Shane's, and it spoke but once. Marshal Brady coughed and sagged. With a sob he fell to his knees; pitched forward on his face.

Weaving left and right Shane's leveled pistol menaced the group. "Anyone here feel like makin' somethin' outa this?"

They stiffened to the drive in his voice. Motionless they watched him with wooden faces.

"Shucks," he said, "ain't Brady got no friends among you?" His gray eyes, so like the smoky sage, rested invitingly on Stone Latham's. "How about you?"

"Don't look at me," Stone Latham said. "I never did like Brady, nohow."

Shane said curtly, "Two of you hombres lug Bill Halleck out of my room. I ain't never accustomed myself to sleepin' with a stiff. An' right now I'm aimin' to get some shut-eye. It won't," he added ominously, "be healthy for any gent to go perambulatin' round my door. I'm a light sleeper an' I'd hate mighty much to be disturbed."

CHAPTER FOUR

BEHIND a door labeled "Private Office," in a room partitioned off beneath the balcony stairs of his establishment and made as sound-proof as his dexterity and the tools he had to work with would permit, Jarson Lume and those who owed him "Boss" sat in grim conference.

An atmosphere of tension hung over this gathering that was not the least bit lessened by the savage scowl on the countenance of Lume himself. Plainly the things which had happened since Shane's arrival in Tortilla Flat had upset his usual impassivity. He paced the floor with nervous stride, hands thrust deep in frock coat pockets.

Stone Latham, cold and cynical, sat at one end of the long plank table toying with a deck of greasy cards. Next to him sat the lithe and slender Puerco, his swarthy face framed by an Indian's mane of black coarse hair, a surly pout on his thick, repellent lips and a bold discoloration at the edge of his receding chin where Shane's hard fist had landed. At Latham's other hand sat Bronc Walders, his restless glance constantly roving about the room. A slouch hat with a chin strap gave him a hard-case appearance that was ominously borne out by the shiny grip of his double-action Colt and the scuffed condition of its holster against the unscratched black surface of his fancy bat-wing chaps.

Jarson Lume abruptly wheeled to face his lieutenants. Determination lay plain in the forward jut of his clean-shaved jaw.

"Gents," he said gruffly, "somethin's got to be done about this drifting gun-slick. He's too damned fast for my peace of mind. We've got to get rid of him and quick. Already he's snuffed Wolf Brady and Halleck. Gents, this Shane has got to go!"

A sneer contorted Stone Latham's cynical face. "Bravo!" he jeered, and grinned as Jarson Lume's cheeks grew dark. "How you figurin' to get rid of him?"

"I wasn't thinking of askin' *you* to gun him," Lume said coldly. Concentration wrinkled his brows as he took another turn about the room. He stopped with his back against the fireplace and hooked his elbows on its dusty mantel.

He said, "I've engaged him to ride shotgun guard to a shipment of gold."

A silence settled across the room and held for a number of moments. Then Latham said, "It won't work. This Shane's too slick to be taken in by that game. You'll have to figure somethin' else. The stakes are too important to run such risk right now."

"There's bound to be a strong element of risk in dealing with a man like Shane," Lume answered. "No way of getting around it. We'll load the strong-box with rock rubble an' start him off. Kettle-Belly Dunn an' his boys will stop the stage at Keeler's Crossing—"

"They'll never cut it," Stone Latham growled. "Shane'll blast that bunch to hell! Mark my words, you've got to think up somethin' better'n that, Lume. This Shane ain't no ordinary leather-slapper. He's got brains an' knows how to use 'em. Ever notice his eyes?"

Jarson Lume's straight thin-lipped mouth grew tight. Through his teeth he said, "I'm figuring to have Wimper ride inside the stage."

Bronc Walders nodded, grinning. "That'll do it. While Shane's busy throwing lead at Dunn's bunch, Wimper can send a blue whistler through his gullet easy as rollin' himself a smoke. Hell, it'll be like takin' candy from a kid!"

But Stone Latham, apparently, was not convinced. He said no more, but the saturnine curve of his lips told plain as words what *he* thought about this plan.

"Well?" Lume snarled, "what's wrong with it?"

Latham made no reply but his shrug was eloquent.

A soft, peculiar knocking on the door at that moment interrupted the business before the meeting. Lume growled, "Come in!" and the door swung open abruptly and as quickly shut behind a short, squatty man with a squint in one eye and a weather-beaten face whose right cheek bulged to an oversized cud of tobacco.

"Well? What is it, Lefty?" Lume demanded.

"I got the dope on that payroll for the Copper King," Lefty Hines announced out of the corner of his mouth. "It's comin' through from Phoenix on the next up-country stage."

A feline sparkle lighted Lume's cold eyes. His companions straightened to attention.

"How many guards they sendin' with it?" Stone Latham asked.

"None!" the newcomer chuckled. "They figger it won't attract no notice if they don't guard it. Figger they'll get it through that way. Yuh know they've allus hired a bevy of shotgun guards on the other trips. When we lifted their last shipment, Obe Struthers said by Gawd he would have to close down if the next shipment didn't get through."

Lume smiled coldly. "How much gold they got stored up there? Stamp mill's been running pretty regular, seems like. They ought to have quite a pile ready to go out."

"They have. Looks to me like this would be a damn fine time to stage a raid."

"Against all them guns they've got scattered around that office?" Stone Latham sneered. "You must have water on the brain!"

"Hell! we could pull it easy," Hines pointed out. "They swap shifts day an' night. All their tough guns are on the night shift. Daytimes there's on'y three fellas guardin' that office. Three fellas an' ol' Obe, himself. Cripes, you couldn't ask for a better lay!"

"Hmmm," Jarson Lume breathed, and took a turn about the room. "We might be able to cut it at that."

"If we got away with that gold," Bronc Walders muttered, "an' stopped their payroll, too, I'm bettin' we could buy Obe Struthers' Copper King Mine for the price of a new hat!"

Hines nodded. Looking curiously at Lume, he said, "I thought yuh gave us boys strict orders to lay off that dame what runs the Come-An'-Get-It?"

Lume's cold immobile face swung toward Hines swiftly. No least ripple of emotion crossed it. "I did." And after a brief pause during which his lambent gaze searched the squatty man's features, he added, "An' I meant it. Lize Corbin's to be left strictly alone, far as this gang's concerned. I made one mistake in that skirt, an' I don't want her riled one damn inch further. One of these days she's gonna be worth money in my pocket."

Hines grinned mirthlessly from a corner of his mouth as his squint-eyed glance passed from Lume to Latham, and from Latham to Puerco. It flicked back to Latham, then, and he said, "I reckon that order don't include Stone Latham, eh?"

Latham grinned as Lume said coldly, "No. Latham's workin' under orders."

"I guessed he musta been when I heard how that driftin' pilgrim handled—"

"That'll be enough outa you!" Stone Latham purred. There was a bold intentness in his glance as his hand dropped suggestively to gun-butt.

"Shucks, Stone, I wa'n't meanin' nothin'," the squatty Hines said easily. "Jest tryin' to get things straight in my think-box, is all. I reckon," he tossed the jeer across the silence carelessly, "Puerco's been workin' under special orders, too?"

There came a fraction of absolute silence; then, through the shredding stillness, Puerco's breath came raspingly and he ran a shaking hand round the collar of his greasy shirt.

Stone Latham, his eyes thin slits, rose slowly from his chair; moved softly backward from the table. The cold, bloodless face of Jarson Lume taut.

Fingering his tiny mustache, Lume drawled, "Just what is the meanin' of that crack?" And his words fell across the hush with the metallic clink of pebbles in a box.

Hines grinned malignantly. "Yuh know that alley between the Warwhoop an' the Jug O' Rum? Well, I happened to be saunterin' past it a while back an' I heard some right peculiar sounds. I stopped. An' right then a curtain in the Jug O' Rum flew up an' lit that alley like the sun was shinin'. I seen a certain gent here wrastlin' with that Corbin dame. He had her shirt half torn off."

"Yeah?"

"Yeah. Well, I didn't butt in, figgerin' 'twas none o' my never-mind. Wa'n't no need of me puttin' in my oar nohow 'cause that stranger what mixed it with Latham an' rubbed Wolf Brady out was headin' for the gal an' this gent like a fire hoss when the third alarm starts ringin'. He wasn't wastin' any words neither, by cripes! He jest waded in an' bounced a coupla haymakers off this gent's chin so quick 'twould make yore haid swim," and Hines looked saturninely at the shrinking Puerco.

"One gah-tham lie!" the Mexican shrilled, kicking back his chair. "I nevair touched thees—"

Bronc Walders' hoarse laugh, like the rest of the Mexican's words, was lost in two smashing reports that burst across the room like towering thunder, beating back against the walls in deafening waves of sound.

Stone Latham and Jarson Lume both stood with smoking guns in hand as Puerco's knees buckled and spilled him, retching blood, across the floor. A wicked snarl was on Latham's lips and Jarson Lume's cold,

43

bloodless face was taut.

Lume said, "The next sport that makes a play at Lize Corbin can expect the same. By Gawd, I'm runnin' this camp, an' it's high time you birds was recognizin' that when I say a thing I *mean* it! Walders, throw that carrion out in the alley."

Sudden Shane had no intention of going to sleep when he shut the door of #10. Nor did he. To be sure, he sat down on the bunk, took off his boots and dropped them heavily on the floor. But—then he quietly put them on again. After that he settled comfortably back against the wall and built himself a smoke.

There was a whimsical light in his sage-colored eyes as he leisurely puffed his quirly. No remorse for the men he had killed was bothering his cogitations. Those men, to his way of thinking, had received exactly what their actions merited. The first man had been loosening the reins of his horse—a trick to lure Shane into a line where the horse-thief's hidden helper could cut him down. That the scheme of this twain had not panned out was hardly any fault of theirs; they certainly had been serious enough. Yes, Shane mused, killing was no more than they deserved. He had been generous and lenient under the circumstances, having killed but one. The bullying Marshal Brady had come asking for what he got. So, too, had the bushwhacking Bill Halleck!

It was Shane's suspicion that the horse thieves had been hired by Lume to rub him out. Halleck, too. But the marshal— Well, Shane was willing to bet considerable that Brady had been sicced on him by Latham.

What, he wondered, was the connection—if any—

between Stone Latham and Jarson Lume? Somehow he had a hunch there was a connection, that Lume and Latham were working hand in glove to part this camp from its gold and copper. And Shane, be it known, was a man who loved to give his hunches the free rein.

His thoughts swung to the man whose scribbled note had brought him to this camp. Obe Struthers, owner of the misnamed Copper King. Shane's lips quirked humorously as he thought of the mine-owner's letter. It had been both brief and pointed; four words—"Business going to hell!"

Struthers had been pretty sure that would bring the man to whom it was sent, Shane reflected. He was probably in a stew right now because the addressee had not shown up.

With a frown Shane's kaleidoscopic thoughts shifted to Lume and Latham again. He had made an enemy of Latham; perhaps of Lume. At any rate, it was beginning to be apparent that the Square Deal's proprietor was not intending to take any chances. A strange gun-slick was better dead.

Shane chuckled softly as he smoked his cigarette. "'There's many a slip 'twixt the cup an' the lip,'" he quoted. "An' the best laid plans have a uncommon bad habit of goin' haywire. Mister Jarson Lume'll find I'm a dang hard gent to kill. If I got anythin' to say about it."

And, sitting there with one foot drawn up on the edge of the bunk and his hands clasped about the knee, he looked very much as though he'd have a whole lot to say about it. He gave off an air of cold efficiency as he set there musing. His eyes, so alike in color to the smoky

45

sage, were serene and tranquil. Though his square-cut features were intensely aquiline, he had a genial mouth and laughing lips that were ever showing his strong white teeth in a way that was mighty attractive, yet did not detract a fraction from his hard look of capability.

He thought of Jarson Lume. The fellow's cold eyes and lips warned him that a man must be cautious in his dealings with him. He had heard, through that grapevine telegraph of western gossip, that few men had ever been on back-slapping terms with Lume. It had been rumored widely how on first arriving in this camp, Lume had gunned out two men's marks over some trivial disagreement. It seemed that Jarson Lume held small faith in the efficacy of Golden Rules. Rumor insisted that a number of the camp's former big men who had crossed Lume in public, had later been rubbed out in private where none had been on hand to prove their passing had been attended by fair play. All that had saved Lume's neck upon these occasions had been the care and secrecy with which the suspected murders had been carried out.

Lume, Shane reflected, was plenty slick.

His thoughts wandered to Lisabet Corbin. His hands clenched tightly as the image of Puerco crossed his mind. The skunk! He'd better keep his paws off Lize or Shane would see that he got an enlightening introduction to Colonel Colt!

Shane had no use for Mexicans, having been raised along the border.

A knock upon the door abruptly terminated his cogitations.

"Come in," he drawled and, rising, dropped his hand to gun-butt.

A girl entered; the frowsy blonde he had seen earlier with Stone Latham.

"Close the door," he said, and crossed his arms, his glance upon her painted face enquiringly.

That she had something to say, was evident; her trouble seemed to be in arriving at a satisfactory opening. After several false starts, she blurted,

"You better clear out of this camp right quick!"

He smiled in a way all his own. "Ah," he said, and blew a cloud of smoke ceilingward. "Nice of you to tell me."

"I'm dead serious. Stone Latham will kill you if you don't!"

Shane appeared calm and indifferent. "I wouldn't let that worry you none, ma'am. After all, I been weaned a week or two an' ought to be trusted to know what I'm doin'. I've been in camps like this before. An' Stone Latham ain't the first of his kind I've had a run-in with. I reckon I'll get along."

She came suddenly toward him where he stood beside the bunk and placed her hand upon his arm. "You're so young," she said. "So young and honest looking. I—I'd hate to see you killed."

Shane grinned at her, coldly. "What's the—" he broke off as a double concussion shook the floor beneath his feet.

The girl caught a hand to her carmined lips; her eyes stared wide and frightened.

"Just some of the boys celebratin', I reckon," Shane

said. "Nothin' to get alarmed about, I expect. Does Latham know you're up here?"

Her hazel eyes reproached him. "Listen," she said, coming closer. "You don't know what you're up against here. Stone Latham—"

"What's the game, kid?" he reached up and caught her hands to ward them off.

She threw herself against him and began to struggle. Her lips parted in a scream that sent tingling chills across Shane's scalp. There was some trick about this business, was the thought that crossed his mind.

And while his hands still gripped her twisting wrists and her body was jammed close against his own, as though to prove his thought correct the door bulged open and across the girl's bare shoulder his eyes met the bold, sardonic stare of Stone Latham.

"Well," Latham breathed, and "*Well!* You damned woman-thievin' polecat!"

Even as Latham's hand sped downward for his gun Shane, with what seemed a miracle of dexterity, flung loose of the cursing girl and slapped his hip.

A visible shudder ran through Stone Latham's raw-boned body and his descending hand was arrested midway in its swooping arc. His widening eyes hung as though fascinated to the black orifice of the pistol which, like magic, had appeared in Shane's right hand.

A cold, mirthless grin framed Shane's white teeth.

"Almost, hombre—almost," he drawled. "But not exactly quite. One of these times I might get a little careless an' your friends'll be luggin' you out on a shutter."

CHAPTER FIVE

T HE sun, gilding in its passing the brazen upthrust crags of the Superstition Mountains, and gilding, endowed them for fleeting moments with cloaks of gold and lilac, was slinking off to bed when Sudden Shane opened his eyes and yawned. Throwing his denim-clad legs across the edge of this bunk that once had been Bill Halleck's, and tugging on his boots, Shane crossed to the open window and stood there looking out and breathing in great pungent drafts of the cooling, invigorating air.

His untroubled glance took in those towering escarpments brooding in slumbrous silence so far above the flimsy structures of this town. Then, drooping lower, his roving gaze took in the gathering shadows that filled this tiny level men called Tortilla Flat. He watched how the drifting gloom rolled in between the buildings, choking the dusty alleys with a thickening murk that even crept insidiously up the frowning cliffs that hemmed this wicked camp.

Night's coming would be swift, he mused. And swifter still would be Death's coming and the sinister slither of his sickle snuffing souls in this place of turbulence and greed, once the darkness fell.

Shane shrugged away the thought and moving from the window turned his attention to a careful inspection of his gun. It did not seem to have been tampered with while he slept, but he could afford to take no chances. Emptying the bullets from its chambers, he replaced

49

them with fresh ones picked alternately from the loops of his wide black belt. Then, holstering the weapon, he pulled his hat low down across his eyes and, opening the door, went out upon the balcony overlooking the bar, gambling layouts and dancing floor beneath.

He stood for some time by the railing, letting his sombre, wary glance play over the sights below. No one needed to tell him that, from now on, the guns of this camp's sporting element would leap from leather to snuff his light with the first opportunity permitted them. Cat-eyed watchfulness and speed incredible was the price of a gunman's life. One careless fraction of a second on his part now would return him to that dust already hiding so many forgotten men. Knowing this his face was grave as he stood there idly contemplating that shifting scene below.

The outsides of the Square Deal's windows now were blackened by the garish light of the fifty coal-oil lamps that were bracketed along its inner walls. Below Shane, streaky stratas of lazy-swirling tobacco smoke drifted above the hatted heads of the variegated throng patronizing the many pleasures offered by Jarson Lume's establishment.

Playing stud at a table almost directly below him, Shane saw the blonde girl who, early this morning, had almost given Stone Latham the chance he was wanting. She was sheathed in some clinging material of pale blue that made alluring contrast to her yellow hair. In the latter, now, she wore a high-backed Spanish comb a-sparkle with imitation gems.

Three men were with her. One was a paunchy gent

whose right hand seemed to love the handle of his gun; another had restless straw-colored eyes, sneering lips and a chin strap on his hat; while the last member of the male trio was a sawed-off man with close-set eyes in a pock-marked visage that was as evil as any Shane had ever seen.

This last-mentioned hombre caught Shane's glance upon them and muttered something under his breath. His companions suddenly looked up. Seeing Shane, the man with the chin strap scowled. Then all three returned their attention to their game. Shane continued to watch them for a while, but finally tired of it and descended the stairs.

He threaded a leisurely way among the gambling tables and thirsty customers headed for the bar. Even in a camp of this sort, he reflected, it seemed a bit unusual for a resort to be so heavily patronized at this early hour. For a time he speculated on the matter while he studied the boisterous throng, but finally gave it up and shoved through the Square Deal's swinging doors.

Night, he saw as he stood beneath Lume's wooden awning, had already veiled much of the sordid ugliness which stamped by day the physical dimensions of Tortilla Flat. But he found nothing beautiful in it even now. This place, he reflected, was a very paradise for outlaws and hunted men of all descriptions. Only one law could function here—the harshly sudden law of Colonel Colt. And listening to the nocturnal sounds about him, he opined that it was a law that functioned regularly.

He became aware that he was hungry and turned his steps through the hock-deep dust toward Lize

Corbin's place.

He noted abstractedly how lights from open doors and windows threw bars and pools of gold across the blue shadows dappling the street, and how the stars high up above him looked like guttering candles in the purple bowl of heaven. But even so, his keen gray eyes were alert to the things around him. Had some pistol-yanker tried to catch him napping, he would have received a surprising jolt. For Texas Shane's reputation as a quick-draw artist had kept him always on his guard against the glory-aspirations of lesser guns. And the habit clung.

He thought again of Struthers as he crossed the busy road. Obe Struthers' pointed note had not been sent to him, but to his brother, who today—had he lived—would have been just eight years older than Sudden Shane. But Jefferson Shane had been killed four years ago by dry-gulch lead. Evidently Struthers had not heard. Struthers and Jeff had once been pardners. So Sudden Shane had come to Tortilla Flat at Struthers' call in his brother's stead. The Shanes had always been noted for things like that; in Texas it was said that when a Shane once called you "friend," he'd fight for you till hell froze over—and then skate for you on the ice. Sudden Shane was a man who believed in keeping up traditions.

When he entered the Come-An'-Get-It he saw that the place was filling up. A good dozen customers bestrode the stools along the oil-cloth covered counter. Taking one of the few still-vacant stools, Shane leaned forward on his elbows and grinned at the bustling girl.

When she got around to it, Lisabet came and stared at him inquiringly. "Well, speak up, stranger. Y'u ain't the only pebble on this beach!"

Shane chuckled. "I'll take some eggs fried sunny-side-up on a raft of ham. An' a cup of java. An' some apple pie, ma'am. How's business? Flourishin'?"

An angry light flared in her stormy eyes. "Good as could be expected—considerin' yo' still hangin' round an' bumpin' off my best customers!" And with an expressive sniff, she went off about her work.

Shane thoughtfully rasped his chin with a lazy finger. "Pretty sassy," he reflected, "considerin' the scrape I got her out of las' night. Reckon that old saw 'bout whistlin' gals an' crowin' hens ain't far from wrong," he concluded enigmatically.

The man on the stool beside Shane gave him a grin. "Can't noways satisfy that dame," he observed through a champing mouthful. "Coldest critter on Gawd's foot-stool, bar none. Even Lume can't get no place with her—an' that's sayin' somethin'."

Shane nodded without comment. So Lume *had* been monkeyin' around! Was he the polecat who had put the sullen resentment in Lize Corbin's eyes?

He reached out and caught the plates and cup she sent slithering down the counter, loaded with his order. He dumped four spoonfuls of sugar in his coffee and began the serious business of "feeding his face."

One by one his companions finished their meals, grabbed toothpicks and sauntered out, leaving their money beneath their plates. He watched the girl clear the dirtied dishes from the counter, disappear with them into the kitchen. When she returned she stopped before him and leaned against the counter, eying him soberly.

"I didn't get a chance to thank y'u for what y'u done last night," she said. "I'm thankin' y'u now."

Shane flushed. "Shucks, ma'am, don't be mentionin' it. I'd have done the same for anybody." And his flush grew hotter as he saw the old resentment flare up in her eyes and realized he'd put his foot square into things again.

"Yes," she said with stormy glance, "I reckon you'd 'a' done it for any—"

But there he cut her off. "Don't say it, ma'am. 'Twouldn't be noways fittin' an', besides, the hard cases round this town that had orn'ry notions have begun to opine as how they mebbe made a mistake in readin' your brand. They're beginnin' to figure mebbe they've had you all wrong plumb from the start. Ain't no sense runnin' yourself down when other folks is startin' to run you up."

"The only reason they're figurin' to run me up is account of y'u. I reckon y'u are some shucks with a gun, Shane. Looks like most of the salty hairpins in this camp is right anxious to keep outa yo' way since y'u downed Wolf Brady an' Wild Bill Halleck. But I ain't allowin' that's helpin' me none. They'll keep theah dirty tongues off'n me all right, when yo' around. But when y'u leave they'll come snarlin' round ag'in. Y'u oughta know a fella cain't make a silk purse outen a cow's hind end."

"You ought to smile when you say that, ma'am. 'F I heard a gent make a remark like that about you, I expect

54

I'd bend my gun on him quick. Shucks," Shane gravely added, "Trouble is with you, ma'am, you're lettin' ancient hist'ry obscure the silver linin' of your cloud."

"Well, the trouble with *y'u* is y'u ain't got sense enough t' know when yo' reached the limit. This sportin' crowd here'll git set right sudden an' *psssst!* Theah'll be a *bammm,* some flame an' a puff of smoke an' y'u'll be plumb washed up an' in yo' coffin! I'm a-tellin' y'u! I've seen it happen befo'. Theah ain't no gent tough enough to buck this camp an' git away with it. Shane, yo' ridin' for a fall!"

Shane only chuckled amusedly. "I reckon not—"

"Jest like all the rest o' the men!" she flashed. "Confident as Billy-be-damned an' plumb stiff-necked as hell! If y'u had any sense, y'u'd git right outa this sink of iniquity an' settle down on some nice quiet ranch an' mind yo' own business."

Shane's eyes twinkled. He had a ranch of his own back in Texas right this minute. But he held his face sober as he looked Lize Corbin in the eye; there was no need of airing the fact, he thought.

"Why, ma'am," he gravely drawled, "I reckon I'm a box-head for not thinkin' of somethin' like that sooner. I'm plumb mortified a lady had to point it out to me."

She regarded him suspiciously, as though sensing laughter in his words. But his face was faintly flushed and showed no sign of mirth.

"Where do you reckon I could get me such a place," he asked, "in case I decide to do that little thing?"

"How do I know? Use yo' ears! Use yo' eyes! Theah oughta be plenty of spreads for sale. Lume an' his tough

55

guns has raised so much deviltry in this country I allow y'u oughta be able to pick up a place right cheap. 'Course the on'y way y'u could keep it stocked would be with a hard-case crew what didn't give a damn for gold-minin'. Everyone round thisaway has done got gold colic bad. Couldn't git 'em to work at no ordinary chore for all hell. I allow theah'll be one hellimonious passle of paupers in this country when this boom curls up."

"Well, ma'am," Shane said, bowing to her and slipping some money under his plate, "I reckon I'll go put my ear to the ground an' see what I can discover along them lines." He glanced at his timepiece. "Yep, I reckon I better be siftin' along."

"I expect yo' better be siftin' quick. Stone Latham is crossin' the street an' he's got company. If y'u an' him is figgerin' to have a ruckus, I'd admire for y'u to have it outside. These fixin's here cost me money."

But he could tell by her strained expression that it was not the fixings she was worried about, but him. She was anxious for him to get away without a meeting with the saturnine Latham. He wondered if she knew about the run-in they'd had this morning in the Square Deal's Room Number Ten. He decided that she didn't, since it would be unlike his conception of Stone Latham for the man to air a thing so greatly to his discredit. This morning Latham had had all the breaks yet his gun had not come out of leather. Either Latham's nerve had snapped at the crucial moment, or native caution had bidden him stay his hand.

Shane looked at the girl. Concern lay plain in the pale

rigidity of her cheeks. For some reason she evidently did not want him to engage Stone Latham in a gun battle. He couldn't see why she should be concerned—unless it was because of what he had done for her, and she feared Latham's friends might throw in too and down him. He dismissed the matter with a careless shrug.

"I can't run away, ma'am. What has to be has to be. This is one of them situations that has to be brazened out. I reckon I'll just wait an' see what they got on their minds."

"Y'u dang lunkhaid!" she flared. "I reckon yo' tryin' to get yo'self killed off!"

"Shucks," he drawled gently, "it's uncommon hard, ma'am, to dodge a shoot-out by hustlin' off. Them fellas'd figure I was aimin' to cut my stick an' they'd put a wrong interpretation on it. They'd—"

"Git killed, then, if it'll be any satisfaction to y'u," she snapped, and flounced back into the kitchen.

Shane grinned ruefully and rasped his jaw. "Sure is a spitfire," he marveled.

But his face grew quickly sober as boots clumped heavily across the board walk outside.

Stone Latham pushed through the door, followed by two other men who crowded on his heels. There were scowls on the faces of the latter, but Latham's features were wreathed in a saturnine smirk.

"Howdy, Shane," was his greeting. "Like to have you meet a coupla friends of mine; Birch Alder an' Shoshone Mell. Boys, this is S. G. Shane."

Shane nodded coolly, but did not offer to shake

hands. "Howdy," he said, and waited, his hands hanging loosely at his sides.

"So y'u are Shane, are y'u?" Staring curiously, Alder drawled, "Y'u are makin' quite a rep."

"It ain't my fault if folks round here wants to commit suicide," Shane said modestly. "I do my best to avoid these things but—"

Alder shot a stream of tobacco juice between his broken teeth. "Humph!" he sneered and, moving forward, climbed upon a stool.

Shane turned a little to keep all three men within his vision. He did not like that "Humph!" of Alder's, nor did he like the fellow's move. It seemed to him just a bit too deliberate, as though the thing had been according to some prearranged plan.

He looked Birch Alder over carefully. He was a solidly built man, muscular, and heavy of face. Years of the wrong kind of thought had drawn a corner of his mouth downward until his coarse features held a perpetual sort of leer. There was a sneaking droop to his big shoulders that spelled "Gunfighter"—an epithet backed by his two bone-handled Colts in tied-down holsters.

The other man, Shoshone Mell, was a lanky, thin-lipped hombre who moved with a slouching shuffle. A cropped black mustache adorned his upper hp which, when taken in conjunction with the tuft of black hair on his chin, gave him a cast of countenance extremely reminiscent of the face of Lucifer. His dark and sunken eyes held smouldering fires in their gleaming depths. And Shane saw notches on the worn handle of his gun.

"Looks like you are travelin' in big-time company,"

Shane said to Latham with a grin.

Latham grinned back felinely. "I always travel in big-time company," he boasted. "Lume still got you on his payroll?"

"No, but he doesn't know it yet. I quit five minutes ago."

A shadow crossed Latham's features but vanished instantly. "A good thing," he approved. "The sooner you get out of this town the longer you'll have to keep on eatin'."

"Ain't nothing the matter with my appetite," Shane said cheerfully.

"There will be if you ain't on your way right quick," was Latham's significant reply. "When you leavin'?"

Shane looked at Latham's two gunfighters an' drawled, "I'm figurin' to leave right now, if it's all the same to you."

"Glad to see you showin' sense," Latham said, and sneered, "I allowed you'd see the light."

"What light?"

"The light my friends here make."

"Shucks," Shane drawled softly. "You wasn't allowin' as how they could *make* me leave, was you? 'Cause if you was, I reckon I'll stay on awhile."

"Aah," Birch Alder sneered, "he's just blowin', boss. Y'u wantin' me to run him out?"

Shane said quickly, "I'd admire to see you try," and his gun gaped wickedly at Birch Alder's middle.

The gunman's mouth fell open in surprise and con-sternation. "Geez," he muttered. "Where'd y'u hev that hid?"

Shane grinned and, like a wink, his gun was back in leather. The movement had been so swift no eye had followed it. Latham's men stared blankly. Latham sneered as Birch Alder asked, in a voice newly tinged with respect, "What'd y'u say yore name was, Mister?"

"Shane—S. G. Shane."

"What's the 'G' stand for?" Shoshone Mell chipped in.

"Gun."

Birch Alder heaved a sigh. "I'll hev to take my hat off to yore speed," he said reluctantly. "Y'u sure are sudden."

"That," drawled Shane with a cold, tight grin, "is what the 'S' stands for."

CHAPTER SIX

IT was said that his mother, a dance hall girl from Deadwood, had died in a drunken stupor while his father was making bets in the Coffin Bar as to how much longer she would last. Certainly young Jarson Lume had been fed quantities of violence with his pap, whatever else may be said either for or against him. His character was the result of wild ancestry, mixed blood, and the turbulent environment of the gold camps and boom towns in which his sire, notorious for his owlhoot exploits, had dragged him up.

No other age or country could have aroused in Lume the rugged force and individuality he had found so necessary to dominate the snarling pack of wolves who brought to him the greater portion of his wealth. In this rough land none but the strongest could survive. That Lume had made himself a leader here, bespoke the man's ruthless efficiency; bespoke, too, a deadly skill in the use of Colt's "persuaders" and an iron nerve that up till now had never faltered.

Yet in these last few days Jarson Lume had noticed a change in himself. He had become aware of a latent sense of caution of which, hitherto, he had not known himself possessed. It was disturbing—very. And it dated, he felt bitterly, from the arrival of this hombre, Sudden Shane!

Jarson Lume's straight thin-lipped mouth twisted venomously as he grimly eyed the circle of men about him He had summoned these lieutenants of his to find if anything had been learned of Shane's movements since he had abruptly left town two days ago. The reports they had given him were lame and entirely inadequate. Stripped of subterfuge and alibi, such discoveries as these brainless fools had made were absolutely valueless. Not a single man of the bunch had any idea where Shane had gone. The fellow had veritably dropped from sight!

"Too bad you birds ain't got any eyes in your heads," Lume lashed them. "To hear you jaspers talk, a gent would think the damn earth had developed a mouth an' swallered him, boots, spurs an' pistol!"

Birch Alder snarled something under his breath and clenched his fists.

Lefty Hines swore softly.

"Mebbe you could do better," Stone Latham sneered.

61

"If you got out an' tried, mebbe you'd work off some of that fat you been gatherin' lately!"

An abashed silence settled tensely down across the room. Through it the men's breathing sounded harsh and rasping while Jarson Lume slowly rose from his chair and faced Stone Latham.

Latham's cheeks went gray, but he stood his ground, the sneer still on his lips.

From behind the towering crags of the Superstition Range the dying sun threw splotches of gold and saffron across the splintery floor, and stained the window glass with lilac. Jarson Lume noted these things subconsciously as he somberly eyed his lieutenant and strove to find the right phrase with which to nip in the bud, so to speak, the flare of mutinous defiance to be sensed in Latham's words, and even more in Latham's tone.

The silence grew so long-drawn as to be almost insupportable before at last Lume spoke. And when he did, his husky voice shoved his words across the hush with the grating rasp of a rusty hinge.

"Latham," he said, "I've killed men for less than that—squashed 'em like I would a scorpion. By rights, I ought to rub you out! An' I would if you wasn't the only man with guts in his belly of all this mongrel breed. Now you clamp a latigo on that tongue of yours, by Gawd, or I'll cut it out!"

Again cold silence crept across the room, and only the mournful soughing of the wind through the cottonwoods outside disturbed it. Hot color flooded Latham's cheeks and a red fog was across his eyes.

But he held his tongue.

And then Bronc Walders' voice ran hurriedly across the stillness:

"Yuh know, I've been thinkin', Chief. . . . This Shane pelican won quite a bit of money before he pulled his stake. Won it at one of the poker tables here. I was playin'. Like I said, I've been doin' a heap of thinkin' since then an' I figger there was a reason why Shane kep' pilin' up the chips."

Lume regarded him steadily. "Spill it."

"Wal," Walders hesitated, glanced uneasily at Stone Latham and abruptly blurted, "Latham's woman was settin' in on that game!"

Lume turned the information over slowly, scanning it from various angles. Suddenly in the dim far reaches of his mind a subtle thought clicked into place. The lambent eyes in the cold, bloodless mask that was his face glowed with a new suspicion as they probed Stone Latham's. "Go on, Bronc. You interest me strangely."

"Wal, as I recall it, Shane won every time that damn blonde hellcat dealt."

Latham took a half step forward, menace in every line of his angular rawboned body, his right hand spread claw-like above his holstered pistol. His bold eyes swam with wrath as they fixed themselves on Walders' grinning face. He opened his mouth in a ripped-out curse:

"You lyin' bastard!"

Lume, watching them, saw the gloating look fade swiftly from Bronc Walders' countenance. A sinister leer took its place as his hand, too, slid hipward. Jarson

Lume swore through locked teeth. "Git your hands away from them damn guns!" he snarled. His snaky eyes glowed with a wicked fury. "The first fool to put his paw to iron'll die!"

Bronc Walders spared him a lightning glance and relaxed, grinning. He had seen the black snout of Lume's derringer leveled with stiff malignance from the gambler's hip and knew that for the present he was safe. Stone Latham was never the man to sign his own death-warrant.

"I'm countin' three, Latham," Lume purred ominously.

With a snarl Latham removed his hand from the proximity of his thigh and the look he snapped at Lume was bitter. "Can't you see what this lousy saddle tramp's up to?" he jeered. "He's tryin' to split us up, to turn one man ag'in' the other. Look at the way he got us to wipe out Puerco!"

Lume shifted his flinty gaze to Walders' face. "Hmm. Just what you mean by that?"

"We don't know," growled Latham, "that what he said about Puerco was true any more'n these lies he's passin' 'bout Gracie. *I* know damn well Gracie wouldn't double-cross us like he's puttin' on!"

"You never can tell what a woman'll do," Lume observed coldly. "Mebbe she didn't pass him the cards to take them pots an' mebbe she did. But one thing's certain—Shane nicked me for eight thousand bucks. Somethin's screwy somewhere!"

"What object could she have to pull a stunt like that?" Latham demanded hotly.

Lume looked at Walders.

Bronc Walders said, "I figger she thought mebbe Shane was figgerin' to gun Latham an' wanted some way to get him outa town quick. I allow she reckoned that if Shane won a pile of jack he'd fan dust pronto." He added pointedly, "He sure fanned dust."

"Why, you orn'ry hound!" Latham snarled. "There ain't no damn two-legged jackass can beat—"

"Sit down!" venom oozed from the husky voice with which Jarson Lume shoved his words across Stone Latham's brag. "Sit down an' git a latigo on that jaw of yours before I bust it plumb off!"

Latham sank sullenly into a chair and glowered at Walders between slitted eyes. The muscles along his jaw stood out like strands of rope. A vein throbbed heavily on his left temple.

When not in the grip of rage or excitement, Jarson Lume took pride in his enunciation and always tried to use words that would do him credit and give him the front of a good education—a thing he had never had. The present occasion was an instance of this vanity.

"Now," he said precisely, looking at Stone Latham, "it was not Walders who gave us that line on Puerco. It was Hines, here, as you'd have remembered had you paused for a moment's reflection. You have an annoying habit of going off half cocked, friend. Now this skirt angle is a thing I mean to go into carefully. There's something uncommon odd about this business—particularly the way in which this fellow, Shane, disappeared. One minute he's here and the next he's gone. Smacks too much of magic. Like his draw.

65

"Alder!" he lifted his voice an octave, but its huskiness remained. "You go tell Gracie I want to see her right away. You'll likely find her in her room upstairs if she's not on duty."

After Birch Alder's muscular body had vanished through the door the stillness, like a wayward schoolgirl, came half-heartedly creeping back, as though fearful of what it would find. Surprised at lack of violence in this abode of sudden death, it curled around the room and settled down among the shadows, adding to the general air of gloom an atmosphere of waiting; a brooding, hushed expectancy that brought cold chills to more than one back as man watched man in narrow-eyed alertness, and Jarson Lume watched all.

It was nearly dark outside. In the room the thickening murk was interspersed at intervals by the glowing points of cigarettes as first one man and then another warmed his lungs with the mellow fragrance of good Bull Durham.

Clumping boots presently approached the door and it was flung open, letting in a long lean bar of light from the lamplit bar beyond. A girl entered with a swish of silken skirt and was swiftly followed by Birch Alder who closed the door behind them.

"Let's have a light here," Lume said curtly.

A pair of matches burst red across the gloom as two men reached for lamps. When they were lit and their yellow radiance had driven back the shadows, Lume fixed his lambent glance upon the girl.

"Well, Gracie, what have you got to say for yourself?"

"What do you mean?" her cheeks were pale and there were deep circles beneath her mascaraed eyes.

"Bronc Walders here suggests that you manipulated the cards the other night so that Shane was able to walk out of here with eight grand of my dinero."

The girl looked at Lume with a haunting fear in her eyes. All color had washed from her face, causing her carmined lips to stand out like a smear of blood.

"That's not so," she whispered, backing away. "I tried every trick I know to break his luck. But he was too slick—he was wise to all my stunts an' a few others besides. When he cashed in—"

Lume purred wickedly, "Are you tryin' to tell me, Gracie, you let a drifting gun-slick outdeal you at your own game?"

"As God's my witness," she cried desperately, "I did my best!" She flashed a glance at Latham, at Walders and whirled wildly upon the gambler. "What's that damned renegade tryin' to do? Turn you against Stone Latham?"

Bronc Walders laughed.

Jarson Lume eyed him coldly. "I don't know what he's tryin' to do," he said, "but I've a notion some sucker in this outfit is tryin' to double-cross me. An' if I catch 'em at it, it's going to be almighty unhealthy for 'em!"

"If you're talkin' to me," Stone Latham sneered, "you can save your breath. If you don't like my style I know plenty other gents that'd jump at the chance to have me with 'em. An' gents who ain't in the habit of pinchin' nickels till the buffalo howls."

Jarson Lume got slowly to his feet and his eyes were ugly. "Are you meanin' to insinuate I'm a cheap spore?"

Stone Latham's lantern jaw thrust forward. "It goes like it lays," he gritted. "I've worked with you a long while here an' there, Jarson Lume. I've done things you couldn't hire another gent to do. I've pulled plenty chestnuts outa your fire. But I've never yet run with an outfit what was so uncommon quick at puttin' another gent in the wrong. This mangy pack of coyotes have been snarlin' round my heels long enough. Either you're callin' 'em off or I'm cuttin' my stick! I ain't used to havin' guys put watchdogs on my trail. 'F you don't cotton to my style no more, put Bronc Walders in my job—he seems to have a right gusty hankerin' for it. I allow 'twould be interestin' to see if he could fill it."

A tense cold stillness shut down and hemmed the tableau in. It was like a scene from a wax museum. Bronc Walders with his restless, glittering eyes and ugly scowl; Latham standing gaunt and moveless with his right hand spread above his gun-butt, full lips crooked in a cynical, defiant curve; Kettle-Belly Dunn with his pate hard eyes and wooden features; short, squatty Lefty Hines with his weather-beaten face bulged about an oversized chew of Brown's Mule; Birch Alder, sneering, ready to back Latham's play; Shoshone Mell, his dark, deep-sunken glance a smoulder of kindling malignance as he slouched beside the door, and Jarson Lume with no more expression on his bloodless, darkly handsome face than might have been read in a sandstone crag.

The blonde Gracie stood with clenched hands, her pleading glance on Latham's face, terrified lest he draw and be snuffed out by Lume's hired killers. And beside her the pock-marked Wimper with his hand about the haft of a knife.

In this situation but a spark was needed to set off the dynamite of flaring passions. And a spark was swiftly furnished; a spark that affected the threatened break and massacre as sandbags do a leaking dike, a spark that fused these mounting enmities and jealousies into a strong united front against the outlander.

The door banged violently open.

The eyes of every person in that room fixed amazedly upon the dusty, panting man who stood framed against the barroom light.

He was a big, huge mountain of a man, with bushy-browed black eyes in a swarthy copper face. He was garbed in the picturesque regalia of the California dons; silk lavender shirt, embroidered waistcoat, red sash, wine velvet-and-silver slash-bottomed trousers. A fine sombrero was pushed far back on his head and secured beneath his pugnacious chin by a buckskin thong looped through a perforated 'dobe dollar. As he stared around at the motionless figures he wiped the sweat from his forehead with the back of a hand, and grinned.

"Buenos noches, amigoes."

Lume's husky voice shoved through the silence, "What are you doing here, Tularosa?"

The Mexican doffed his sombrero in a rakish bow to the girl, then stood twirling it by its chin thong as his eyes held those of Jarson Lume. "I tell you, senor,

69

sometheeng 'as 'appen' that makes me of the heart sad—yes, ver-ry. I am come for tell you of eet."

"Well, get on with the tellin'," muttered Bronc Walders, and got an enigmatic look from Latham and a scowl from Tularosa.

Lume said, "Yes. We're busy here."

"Beezee, eh? Wal, you weel be more beezee w'en I tell you some damn fool have bought our ranch at Keeler's Crossing—"

"What!" cold fury was concentrated in that single word Lume drove at the grinning Mexican.

"Si, some Tehanno 'as bought the place for the back taxes. *Seguro si.* It ees the trut'."

Latham asked, "The Keeler's Crossin' spread we use for lettin' the brands heal on our rustled stock?"

The Mexican bobbed his head, still grinning.

Bronc Walders' eyes got smoky and threatening. "An' you let 'im move in, I reckon. What's so damned funny?"

"Fonny?" Tularosa shrugged with Latin grace and spread his hands. "I'm theenk you weel call it the one damn good joke w'en I tell you that thees hombre who bought the rancho, she's fella called Shane. An' I'm theenk you weal laugh som' more w'en I say that thees Shane tell me Senor Lume ees-w'at-you-call setteeng heem up in beeznez."

Gracie swore in a most unladylike manner. "He told me when he cashed his chips that night he was aimin' to buy himself a ranch!"

An oath formed on Stone Latham's compressed lips. "Sure," he stared at Lume. "I told you that pelican was smart! You see what he's done? He's beat this place out of a grubstake an' for back taxes, that *you* insisted we shouldn't pay, he's bought the key ranch in our relay string and at one move thrown a spoke in our wheel that'll put us plumb outa business as far as cattle are concerned until we pry him loose!"

Jarson Lume took one long step that brought his face within inches of Stone Latham's. He snarled, "Shut your mouth, you loose-jawed fool! You tryin' to tell the whole damn' Flat? I'm runnin' this show an' I don't need no advice outa you!"

He whirled on Tularosa as Latham's cheeks went pale with anger. "You," Lume jabbed the Mexican's chest with a rigid finger, "take Wimper an' burn the wind gettin' back to Keeler's Crossin'." His cold eyes flashed about the group and finally settled on Kettle-Belly Dunn.

"Dunn," he snapped, "you c'rral your boys an' follow Tularosa. I want that meddlin' slat-sided Shane rubbed out. I don't want to see any of you birds round the Flat again till you can bring me back his scalp!"

CHAPTER SEVEN

SUDDEN Shane had bought his ranch in haste and now was finding ample time on his hands for repentance. This spread at Keeler's Crossing, he had found after buying it sight unseen, was in need of considerable repair. There was work enough in sight to take care of a full crew of cowboys. And he was finding now what Lize Corbin had pointed out to him when suggesting he buy a ranch—that punchers in this country at this time were scarcer than crow's teeth on the Painted Desert.

He had managed to pick up one man on a hurried trip to Globe. But the fellow had such a hang-dog cast of countenance that he looked more like a surly stage-robber than he did an honest hand. He gave his name as Alibi Smith and said he'd answer to it. Looking him over, Shane had opined Smith had corraled the habit of excusin' himself soon's he'd stepped out of the cradle.

"But dang it, I hev to!" Smith had expostulated. "Folks take one good look at me an' start sprinklin' salt on every word I say. Hell, if I could sue my pan for libel I'd be one of the richest men in the country! I can't hold no job down, nohow. An' I'm a A-1 worker, too! Every time somethin's missin' round a place folks jest nacherly paw my duffle over to see did I hook it!"

Shane chuckled at the recollection. He and Smith were seated beneath the strip of wooden awning which served the adobe shack ranch-house as a porch. It was nearing noon of a hot day. Smith had just knocked off working on the corral which, like everything else about the place, was in need of attention.

"I reckon," Shane observed, looking interestedly at his new hand, "that your life, Smith, must have had a lot of ups an' downs, eh?"

"Wal," Smith scratched his head, then pulled his hat down low above his eyes and wrinkled his long nose. "I dunno about the ups, but I allow I've had a heap more downs than usually falls to the lot of mortal man. Mr. Shane, I've shore had a powerful lot of downs."

"Durin' some of the down periods of your life," Shane commented slyly, "I s'pose you have met up with a number of hard-case characters."

"Wal," Smith rubbed his nose reminiscently, "a few that was tolerable hard," he admitted cautiously.

"I've got to get more men," Shane confided. "I've got a notion they'll have to be pretty tough to do me any good. I'm expectin' a young war round here most anytime. I— Who's that comin' over there?"

Smith looked the way Shane pointed and saw a horseman splashing across the creek. The stranger seemed in no apparent hurry, yet he was moving right along and appeared to be heading directly toward them. "It ain't no hairpin *I* ever seen before," Smith denied.

As the stranger neared them Shane looked him over from head to foot. He looked thin as the brand on the Fence Rail cattle, and he was angular and blessed with protruding front teeth that seemed constantly trying to pry his lips apart. He had an Adam's apple so prominent that Smith felt moved to confide in Shane:

"Looks like a dang baseball had got stuck in his craw!"

The stranger pulled in his horse a few paces off and sat looking down at them curiously. Then abruptly his glance swung to Smith and glowed with the venom of an adder.

"That there bump yer a-lookin' at, Mister, is all there is left of the larst bloke wot made a narsty remark abaht my afflickshun. I'm some'at tender on the subjeck as yer'll bloody well find out if I 'ear any more aspershuns

73

flung in my direckshun!"

Shane looked from the newcomer to the gaping Smith and was hard put to repress a chuckle. He did not know which of the two seemed the more villainous looking, Smith or the funny-talking stranger. Smith's jaw abruptly shut with a clack of teeth and he returned the horseman's glowering stare with interest.

"Aw, go roll yore hoop," he sneered. "A fella thin as you are couldn't scare my shadder—let alone me."

On the heels of this defiance there came the crack of a pistol and dust jumped from the adobe wall between Smith's fingers. He jerked his hand away with a startled oath and his eyes grew big and round as he saw the pistol in the horseman's hand and the tiny wisp of smoke curling lazily from its muzzle. The fierce look was still on the stranger's homely countenance as he swung his glance to Shane.

Shane said, "Nice shootin', pardner. What's your trade when you ain't vacationin'?"

The stranger twirled his gun by the trigger guard as he let his eyes play over Shane. "Hit ain't none of yer bloody business," he said insolently, "but I don't mind tellin' yer I'm a trigger-slammer on which yer can smell the brimstone from hell's backlog! An' 'oo might yer be to be arskin' all the questions?"

Shane laughed and said, "Shucks, I'm S. G. Shane—"

"The bloke that feller Lume's got 'is knife out for?"

"Well," admitted Shane, rasping his chin, "I don't know as Lume's whettin' up his knife for me but somebody surely is."

"Yer said it!" applauded the scrawny stranger. "'E's

74

'ad some flyers 'oisted fer yer—I seen 'em. 'E's got 'em plarstered orl over Tortilla Flat! 'One thousan' dollars reward fer the capture, dead or alive, of S. G. Shane, wanted fer the killin' of Marshal Brady!' "

Shane was perturbed at this unwelcome news, but did not let it show upon his face. Fast work, he was thinking grimly. But aloud he said, "Shucks, it looks like Jarson Lume is gettin' rightdown reckless with his money. Was you aimin' to collect it, stranger?"

The stranger spat significantly. "Bless me, no! A fine mug I'd be to 'elp 'im out, wot? 'Im that 'ad me pinched an' fined fer runnin' a bit of a crap game out in front of 'is blarsted Square Deal! Blimey! I tell yer straight, Mister, if that bloody marshal 'adn't took me rod awy I'd 'ave punctured 'is mortal tintype, s'elp me!"

It came to Shane as he studied this curious fellow thoughtfully, that here was a brand for the burning. Always providing of course that Lume had not discovered his whereabouts and was seeking to install this queer fire-eater among Shane's outfit as a spy. But that, to Shane, seemed hardly likely for he felt that had Lume located him he would have dispatched some gun-slicks swiftly with orders to put an end to him. And, since Shane had not seen this fellow during his stay in town, it seemed reasonable to suppose the man was, like himself, a stranger among the Philistines.

He said, "But you've got a gun now."

"I sure 'ave!" admitted the horseman most emphatically. "An' I won't be back'ard abaht usin' it. Not 'arf."

"Care to take on a job?"

75

The stranger looked suspicious. "That sounds a bit like work, Mister," he opined. "Work's like soap—fer them as likes it. Still . . ." he appeared to hesitate, then finally added, "If wot yer got in mind could be described as a contemplated meanness ter that Lume jarsper, I'm all fer it," and he grinned in a peculiar twisted manner.

"I allow Lume an' me is apt to have a run-in sooner or later," Shane agreed. "Someone is certain sure tryin' to lift my hair, an' I wouldn't be none surprised to learn it was Brother Jarson or Friend Latham. You ride with me an' you'll go places, fella—fast."

"Yus," the stranger nodded. "But there's plyces where a bloke mightn't give a damn ter go. I don't aim ter git where I'll be shovin' up the daisies."

"Well, of course, there's that possibility," Shane admitted. "But I think I can promise you plenty of fun before your harp gets handed down. What do they call you, friend?"

"Bless Jones."

"Well, I'm glad to know you," Shane said gravely, shaking hands with the scrawny horseman.

Smith squinted up at him. "Bless? That's a helluva name!"

"Yer wantin' ter make so'thin' out of it?" Jones demanded, glowering.

Smith backed water quickly. "I was jest expressin' a opinion—nothin' pers'nal."

"Better not be!" Jones revealed his buck teeth in a scowl. "'Orace, me ol' man christened me. Hit's a 'andle I ain't never overworked. Wot's *yer* name, pal?"

Smith flushed and looked uncomfortable. He swallowed with apparent difficulty and licked at his lips as though they scorched. He was plainly mortified as he reluctantly admitted faintly, "Albert Percival, but it ain't my fault."

Shane chuckled. Horace and Albert Percival! More ludicrous names for such a pair of hard-case characters he would have been hard put to imagine.

Smith muttered under his breath and his cheeks flamed darkly.

Jones looked positively murderous as, dropping a hand to gun-butt, he snarled:

"Wot the bloody 'ell yer laffin' at?"

Shane's laugh deepened. Then, sobering to a wide grin, he remarked, "Parents sure ain't got no sense of decency when it comes to wishin' names on their kids. The kind we got forces a gent to become a leather-slappin' hell-bender in order to keep from gettin' trampled on. I was awarded Shelley Garrimonde Shane!— but don't never tell nobody!"

The others guffawed loudly and the ice was broken. Shane got out a bottle and friendship was cemented. Jones announced abruptly, "Comp'ny comin'. Bit of dust cuttin' this way fast. Over by that red butte. Yer'll see it in 'arf a sec."

Shane, peering beneath a shading hand, said, " 'Light down an' rest your saddle, Jones. I'm offerin' you the foreman's bunk. Smith here answers to the call of 'Alibi.' "

Presently Shane saw the dust cloud Jones had mentioned. It was speeding nearer fast. "Fella's crazy to be crowdin' a hoss like that in this heat."

"Some blokes ain't got no sense," Jones remarked. "Not 'arf."

"Right," Smith growled, looking covertly at Jones. "Some is born dumb an' others works hard to get that way."

Jones, not catching the look, sniffed. He was holding his glance on the speeding rider ripping up the yellow dust. "That bloke is makin' real lather," he grunted, biting off a ragged chew from a chunk of Star Plug.

Smith eyed the plug and a wistful look crept into his gaze. But Jones put the remainder in his pocket without further ceremony. "Yus—makin' real lather, 'e is. Wonder wot 'e wants?"

"Stick around a spell an' mebbe you'll learn—if yore hoss don't cave in beneath yore rugged weight in the meantime." Smith's tone had an edge of sarcasm but Jones only sniffed and kept his saddle.

"Some blokes' tongues is allus waggin'," he observed, "but they don't never say nothin' fer a grown man ter listen at."

"Why, it's a kid!" Shane muttered, still eying the oncoming rider. "Mebbe someone's chasin' him."

"Naw—we'd 'a' seen their dust if there was."

"Blimey! It's a greaser kid!" Jones muttered after a moment.

A short time later the Mexican youth pulled his horse up on its haunches three feet from the men before the ranch-house, showering them with dust and pebbles. His dark eye sped from one to another of the three, perturbed.

"Senor Shane?"

"Right here," drawled Shane stepping forward.

The youth fumbled in a pocket of his ragged chaps and brought forth a scrap of dirty paper which he extended.

"For Senor Shane," he said and, whirling his horse, was off before a protest could be voiced.

"Yer think I better storp 'im?"

"No, let him go," Shane said, unfolding the paper the youth had given him. "He's just a messenger . . ." His voice trailed off as he took in the single line of scrawled writing that crossed the paper's center. With frowning brows he read it aloud:

" 'Lume is sendin' some hell-benders after yore scalp.' "

There was neither salutation nor signature.

Jarson Lume chuckled deep down in his white throat as he looked at Stone Latham in his office under the balcony stairs in the Square Deal. The usually inscrutable Jarson was feeling well pleased with himself for he felt that he had done a neat stroke of business in tacking up those rewards for Shane, on the heels of sending Tularosa, and Kettle-Belly Dunn after the outlander's scalp.

"Why don't you grin, dammit?" he asked. "We've got that salty Shane fellow sewed up so tight now it would take dynamite to break him loose."

"Well," Latham said sourly, "he's dynamite, all right. Don't never doubt it."

"Why all the pessimism?" Lume scowled at his chief lieutenant. "If Tularosa, Dunn, Wimper an' the rest of that bunch ain't able to stretch that pelican's hide, we can rest secure in the knowledge that one of these reward-hungry townsmen will pot him sure."

"Yeah? Mebbe!" Latham gave a silent laugh, like an Indian. "You are slick, Jarson. I'm allowin' that. But you're not up to standard this last week or two. You're gettin' rattled. Neither Tularosa or Dunn or their men will ever bring you Shane's scalp. Neither will these fool townsmen. Shane will outsmart you again. You wait an' see. You got to get up hell's-fire early to get ahead of that hombre."

Lume's scowl grew dark. "You got somethin' better to suggest?"

"No—an' that's the hell of it. I admit he's got me stumped. Thought I had him sure the other night; I had things all fixed an' he walked right into the trap an' out again, cool as you please. He's got guts, Shane has. You got to hand it to him. An' he's hellimoniously fast with that smoke-pole he packs."

"A curly wolf!" Lume sneered.

"A curly wolf!" Stone Latham spoke very solemnly.

"Cripes," Lume growled. "The fella's human, ain't he? Bullet'll cut him down as quick as the next, won't it? Then what's so damned tough about gettin' him?"

"Who's goin' to stand up to him an' fire the bullet?"

"What's the matter with bushwhackin' him if he's so damned fast?"

"Nothin'—but I wouldn't want that job."

"You are getting uncommon particular, Stone Latham."

"I'm gettin' sense," Latham grinned. "Bushwhackin's

gettin' damned unpopular round this town. We'll be gettin' the troops in here, or the rangers, if we don't watch our step. Where the hell would we be then? I tell you, we've got to take this business slow an' figure every inch of the way. There's a rumor round now that some of these damned miners an' prospectors are goin' to form a vigilance organization. You know what that'll mean!"

"Listen," Lume said huskily. "Listen, Latham! We've got to get rid of this Shane quick. We can't afford to wait! How do we know he ain't a ranger himself, pokin' round to get the goods on us? He's here for some damn reason; he ain't no common drifter."

"You are right about that." Latham studied the wet rings left on the table by bottles and glasses. "I'll see what I can do."

"We better get the hell outa here," Alibi Smith muttered nervously. "If we wait for them hairpins to git here, we might be given jobs pushin' up the daisies!"

"Blimey, yer a odd bloke!" sneered Jones unpleasantly. "Bless me if I don't believe yer wear yer rubbers w'en it rains!"

"I got a sense of proportion, that's all," Smith said defiantly. "What the devil good'll it do anyone for us to stay here an' get murdered?"

"Aah! Did yer ever storp ter think yer might do a bit 'ave murderin' yerself?"

Smith looked uneasy. "I wouldn't want to have to kill a man," he muttered.

Shane looked at him and grinned. "Well, that's a good

Christian sentiment," he opined. "But when fellas like this Tortilla Flat crowd won't play accordin' to the rules, an' insist on stackin' the deck—why, then it's time to raise your foot an' scatter their teeth on the sidewalk."

"Wot yer goin' ter do?" Jones asked.

Shane's smile was whimsical. "Why, boys, I'm fig-urin' to set right here an' greet 'em with the hand of friendship when they come."

"An' if they spit in yer 'and," Jones questioned slyly, "will yer turn the other cheek?"

"Now I'll tell you, Bless. My calculations ain't got that far as yet. But—if these fellas get *too* obnoxious, I reckon it might be a good idea if we took 'em down a peg."

CHAPTER EIGHT

As he rode through the blue silver of the waning night, bent upon the mission Lume had given him, the burly Tularosa's chin sagged forward on his chest and his eyes became mere squinting slits behind the smoke spiralling from the cornhusk cigarro hanging straight from his thick red lips. Tularosa was communing with himself and his thoughts were far from pleasant.

It was a miserable thing, he was telling himself, that a dog of a gringo like Jarson Lume could snap his fingers and watch men jump to obey his wishes. It was extremely distasteful to think that he himself was one of those who jumped. More, it was damnable—surely all the devils in hell were laughing!

What had this Jarson Lume that he himself did not have? Brains? *Pah!* He had brains enough to fill two such skulls as the head of the grasping Lume. Guns? *Christo,* he had as many guns as Lume, and men who were as quick to use them.

He scowled at the black mass of horsemen riding about him. It was very quiet; only the jingling of spurs and the creaking of saddle leather and the muffled beat of the ponies' hoofs disturbing the eternal stillness that is ever associated with Arizona nights. In the far distance a coyote's howl rang thinly.

Tularosa asked himself why he should be risking his life against a man like Shane because Lume had issued certain orders? What was Lume to him? Nothing—less than nothing! A damned dog of a slave driver who squeezed the last drop of profit from all transactions before throwing his men the empty pulp, as a man might toss a bone to a pack of mongrel dogs!

Over his shoulder he sent a glance at the double line of steeple-hatted horsemen riding behind him with the moonlight glistening on their rifle barrels and their crossed belts of gleaming shells. His countrymen, all but two. He shifted his gaze to one of the latter, the paunchy dealer in wet cattle who was riding beside him, Kettle-Belly Dunn.

To himself Tularosa sneered. This Dunn was a witless fool, a plodding clod content to carry out Lume's orders all his life instead of using what brains he had been endowed with to advance his position in life.

Carramba! He—Manuel Tularosa—was a man of vision, a man who could see a vaster profit in this enterprise with himself as the directing genius. He asked himself why he should not take the bit between his teeth and permanently take over the command of this rabble riding in his wake? *Madre de Dios!* it was certainly an idea.

But this dog of a Dunn—what of him? Would he lend his support to Tularosa's plan? He touched Dunn's arm, spoke soft, suave words close to the gringo's ear:

"For many nights we haff worked for the Senor Lume, my frand. What do we haff to show for thees so-dangerous labor, eh? Theenk of the larger profit we could make if we were working for ourselves. *Car-ramba!* there would be no limit to our power!"

Dunn vouchsafed him a sour glance and spat from the far corner of his mouth. "Yeah? An' what would Jarson Lume be doin'? D'ye think he'd be sittin' round twiddlin' his fingers?" He sneered derisively. "Don't be a fool!"

"*Sangre de Dios!*" Tularosa snapped his fingers contemptuously. "The Senor Lume does not own Manuel Tularosa! Who ees thees grasping gringo that we should jomp through the hoop for heem? Thees Shane ees dangerous hombre. I haff talked weeth heem. Would you weesh for die, senor?"

"Hell, death's the common lot," sneered Dunn. "When my time comes shovin' round the bend, I expect I'll go out like I've lived—with my boots on an' a gun in my paw."

"*Si*, thees Shane weel keel you sure! Thees Shane ees—"

"Hell, he ain't so much," Dunn sneered. "Quit frettin'

about him. We got plenty of men to wipe him out. What's eatin' on yuh?"

"Plenty. I do not like thees dog of a Jarson Lume. I do not like the way he combs hees hair; I do not like hees black mustache, nor hees flinty eye. In short, my frand, I do not like heem a-tall! I am not the peon to be driven like the plough-horse! I, Manuel Tularosa, am a man of vision, a man of brain, a—"

"What a hombre," chuckled Dunn derisively.

"You are right," said Tularosa felinely. "I am a man of guts. I say we should thumb the nose at Jarson—"

"An' I say," began Dunn belligerently, and stopped with a choking sob as Tularosa's right hand swung forward like a striking adder and sank a knife to the hilt in his left breast.

"What you say don' matter, frand," grunted the Mexican withdrawing his blade and wiping it on Dunn's vest.

A moment later Dunn reeled and toppled headlong from the saddle. Tularosa held up his hand for a halt and the double line of bandits stopped their horses. The nearer men stared at Tularosa curiously. They had no love for the fat gringo he had stabbed, but were unable to comprehend the killing and were filled with a vague uneasiness.

Tularosa's white teeth flashed in his copper face as he threw the reins of Dunn's pony to a steeple-hatted rider.

"My frands," Tularosa said, "we are no longer fools to be led by the nose. Lume thees, Lume that—all the time Lume, Lume, Lume! From here out we work independently, robbing whom we please an' dividing the entire spoils among ourselves. I, Manuel Tularosa, shall lead you to amazing riches, to wealth uncountable. To hell weeth the gringo peeg!"

"Viva Tularosa! Viva Tularosa!" rang the shouts, and he who shouted loudest was the renegade gringo, Wimper, and the jet eyes glowed in his pock-marked face. Kettle-Belly Dunn had been his closest friend.

In the scantily-furnished office of the Copper King Mine, old Obe Struthers peered grimly at the weather-beaten features of Lefty Hines over the rims of his tortoise-shell glasses. His wrinkled face showed lines of worry; the knuckles of the hand that gripped his desk gleamed whitely in the feeble glow of the flickering candle.

"So Lume is planning to stop the payroll I've got comin' through on tomorrow's stage, is he? The dirty skunk!"

"He'll stop it, too," Hines told him curtly, and spat an amber stream at the brass cuspidor in the corner. "He's out to break you, Obe, jest like he broke Milt Badger an' Ross Clark. He's had his eye on the Copper King ever since we drove that shaft on the sixty-foot level. He knows what we've got down there an' he means to have it. Somebody slipped him a chunk of that ore!"

"But they couldn't! I've had the men searched ev'ry time they went off duty! They haven't—"

"You didn't yank their tongues out, did you? Well, men'll talk, an' someone talked to Lume. I can't tell you how he got that chunk of ore, but I can tell you this—it came from the Copper King, an' it came from that shaft on the sixty-foot level!"

Struthers' face seemed to take on ten years of age. His shoulders drooped, his chin sagged forward on his chest and he stared unseeingly across his littered desk. He roused suddenly with a desperate snarl:

"The damned two-legged polecat! Ain't there nothin' that'll stop him?"

A faint sardonic grin tugged at the corners of Hines' tight mouth and a light of mockery swam in his lidded glance. But he took care that old Obe Struthers did not note these signs of his wolfish amusement. "It's hell, I reckon," he said unemotionally, "but we got to face the facts. Jarson Lume is runnin' this camp an' what he wants he gets. Seems like it would be better to give in an' sell out at the price he's offerin'—"

"Never!" Obe Struthers gritted, half rising from his chair.

"That's a long time," Hines remarked. "You better reconsider, don't you reckon?"

Obe Struthers did not reply to that but hunched deeper in his chair. His tired old gaze passed over the littered papers on the desk and sought the gunbelt and holstered weapon depending from a peg above it, cobwebbed and covered with dust. For a fleeting instant there was a brightening flicker in his eyes. Then it spluttered out leaving them dull and inexpressibly weary.

These things did not escape the wary Hines and contempt lay open on his cheeks. A mirthless humor lighted his stare as the harsh crunch of booted feet on the gravelled earth outside galvanized the old man to a tense rigidity.

"What's that?" he cocked his shaggy head to one side in an attitude of listening. "Somebody comin'?"

A faint smile crossed the gunfighter's mocking lips. "Sounds like it."

Struthers, rising from his chair, was reaching for his gun when the door opened quietly and Jarson Lume's black-frocked figure entered. He closed the door behind him casually and nodded to the mine owner.

"How's tricks?"

"You know damn well they're rotten," Struthers grunted, sinking back in his seat without touching the holstered gun. "An' you know why they're rotten, too! Lume, you're a polecat!"

Lume chuckled. "No secret about that," he said, taking a cigar from his pocket and lighting it. "I've come over here to make you a final offer. Ten thousand dollars for the Copper King. You can take it or you can leave it, Struthers—but I'm advisin' you to take it. You ain't got long to live an' you might's well enjoy what time is left."

Struthers seemed about to let himself go in a violent rage; seemed about to give vent to the terrible hate he held toward this man. He half started from his chair again but sat down heavily when Lume's left arm swept out and brushed the weighted gunbelt from its peg. The thud it made as it struck the floor somehow drew Struthers' eyes to Hines. The gunfighter's red-rimmed eyes had shrunk to slits and he stood in a crouch with right hand poised like a talon above his pistol. His head seemed sunk between his squatty shoulders; his lips were twisted in a wanton smile and his left cheek was white from pressure where his oversized chew bulged against it.

Obe Struthers winced as he looked from Hines to the coldly-grinning Lume.

"So Hines is in it, too," he sighed.

"Hines," Jarson Lume remarked, "is a man who knows which side his bread is buttered on. You'll do better runnin' with the wolves, Obe." He fingered his tiny mustache. "Virtue may be its own reward, like they say in the copy-books, but it takes hard cash to buy good whisky. How about it? My time's valu'ble. You goin' to sell or ain't you?"

Obe Struthers knew when he was licked.

"It'll never work!" declared Alibi Smith, rubbing his long nose energetically.

"Blimey, but 'e's cheerful as a 'angman's grin!" Jones hooted. "A reg'lar ray of sunshine!"

Shane looked at them and chuckled. "Oh, it might. I allow it's sure worth tryin' anyway." He eyed the nose that Smith was rubbing. It was the fellow's most outstanding feature; long and slender with a bony hump in its middle and an upward twist to its end. "You want to be right careful of that proboscis, Smith. It's the only one like it in seventeen counties."

Jones guffawed. But Smith scowled gloomily; he was touchy about his features. "There yuh go," he growled. "Runnin' down my anatomy instead of concentratin' on the details of that crazy scheme you're set to pull. What kinda flowers yuh want in case they're decent enough to bury yuh?"

"Listen at 'im!" Jones exclaimed. "Hell, we'll live ter tell whoppers ter yer gran'children!"

"Not if I know Jarson Lume, yuh won't," Smith sighed lugubriously. "When it comes to butchers he's the real McCoy an' he can hate worse an' longer than sixty-five Injuns. No kiddin'—you fellas better lay off that fast one."

Jones snorted. "Runnin' a sandy on that blighter will be sweeter'n kissin' the Queen of Sheba! I can just see 'is jaw boggin' down an' 'is eyes a-gogglin' when 'e finds out 'ow we've rooked 'im!"

"An' I can jest see yore mootilated corpses after his gunnies gits after yuh!" mourned Albert Percival Smith with a flip at his long skinny nose.

Six days had passed since the Mexican lad had practically foundered a horse to bring Shane that anonymous warning note. Six days during which no faintest sign of danger had distorted the routine life on the ranch at Keeler's Crossing. Growing restive with the dry monotony of bucolic existence, Sudden Shane had hatched up a plan by which he and Bless Jones aimed to deduct a bit of profit from the heretofore smoothly running business of the infamous Jarson Lume.

Alibi Smith shook a mournful head and Shane and Jones saddled their ponies.

"Cheer up, ol' undertaker," grunted Jones. "We ain't never been planted yet."

Smith rubbed his long proboscis. "There's allus a first time for everythin'," he sardonically pointed out. He directed a solemn stare at Shane. "Don't yuh reckon it'd be wise to deed this place to me in writin'—case yuh never git back alive?"

But Shane only chuckled, and presently he and Jones rode off.

"Y'u git outen here, y'u dang chicken hawk!" Lize Corbin gritted, reaching down one hand for the sawed-off shotgun which she kept beneath the counter.

"You can leave that scatter gun where it is," sneered Jarson Lume. "I'm not going to bite you. Just drifted over to ask if you'd heard the news."

"What new— *Never mind!* I ain't interested in no news *y'u* could bring me. Git outen here now 'fore I lose my temper an' blow yo' middle plumb to glory!"

"Cussed if I don't believe you'd do it, too," Lume murmured in admiration.

"Yo' dang right I'd do it—an' I sure will if y'u don't haul yo' freight!"

"Well," the gambler boss of Tortilla Flat said, making as though to leave, "if you ain't interested in that driftin' gun-slick hellion what took up for you against Stone Latham—"

"What?"

"Oh, interested now, eh? I thought Shane's name'd fetch you. Well, you can figure the next time you set eyes on him he'll be where he won't be doin' no more meddlin' with things that don't concern him."

He eyed her over insolently. "I got a tip Shane's been seen over round Youngsburg. I passed the news on to the boys. They saddled up pronto an' hit the trail allowin' they'd be packin' Shane's hide back here before tomorrow mornin' or bust a gut. Ain't nobody left round town but Pedro Abrilla—that is, nobody else but some drunken miners an' a handful of barflies. Nobody's around that'll have any special interest in *you*."

"What y'u gettin' at?" Lize Corbin lifted her scatter gun and placed it handy on the counter. "Yo' wolf-pack'll never git Sudden Shane—he's a heap too smart for the likes of y'u! Y'u roll yo' hoop outen here now or I'll smoke y'u up sure as Gawd makes little apples!"

"That ain't no way to talk to your—" Lume grinned mockingly, "to the fellow who's goin' to be your husband inside the next hour."

"Husband, hell!" Lize Corbin snapped with unlady-like emphasis. "I wouldn't marry y'u, Jarson Lume, if y'u was the las' white man on earth! I'd sooner be married to a sheep-dipped herder than to hitch up with a two-legged skunk like y'u. Why, yo' so dang low a snake's belly would pass clear over the top of yo' haid!"

A queer smile curled the lips of Jarson Lume. "Still feelin' proddy about that little affair of ours, eh? Well, I've seen my mistake, Lize, an' I'm plumb anxious to marry you now. I'm—"

"Yeah! Y'u are plumb anxious to marry the gold mine y'u think my ol' man found before y'u bumped him off!" she jeered, her stormy eyes flashing over him contemptuously. "Y'u better clear outen here now before Shane finds out what yo' up to. He'd knock y'u so far it would take a blood-houn' a week to find y'u!"

Lume chuckled silently. "Shane ain't goin' to be in no condition to knock anything once the boys get their sights lined on him. He's all washed up. An' so will you be—unless you're willin' to listen to reason. Hell, girl, it ain't every skirt I'd ask to marry me! Get hep to yourself, Lize. Any bit of fluff in town'd jump at the chance to get a man like me—"

"Well, here is one bit that ain't figurin' to do no jumpin'!"

Lume's handsome, bloodless face abruptly darkened with rage. "No?" he snarled. "Well right there's where you're mistaken, girl. Grab 'er, Pete!"

Whirling, like some frightened animal, Lize Corbin saw behind her the swarthy grinning face of Pedro Abrilla. Cat-like, he had entered through a window in the kitchen and softly stalked upon her while she stood listening to the husky-toned voice of Lume. As Abrilla sprang she reached for the shotgun, but her fingers closed on empty air. Jarson Lume had snatched the weapon even as she reached.

"Call off yo' wolf," she panted, struggling in Abrilla's bear-like arms.

"You agreein' to marry me?" drawled Lume with a mocking grin.

"No I ain't!"

"Better treat her a little rougher, Pete," Lume advised. "She'll take a lot of gentlin'."

"Y'u damned coward!" the girl cried bitterly. "Y'u wait'll Shane—"

Lume sneered, "Shane won't be botherin' anyone any more. You better give in. One way or another I'll have you anyway. Whether you like it or not you're goin' to marry me this afternoon—"

93

"Y'u won't get no preacher to marry me against my wishes!" Lize panted, kicking at the Mexican's shins.

"Don't count too heavy on that. There's lots of ways of makin' a man do somethin' he don't have no natural inclination for. There's a sky-pilot in the jug right now that I've been holdin' since yesterday for just this purpose. Coupla the boys roped him on the trail to Mormon Flat an' I had Latham arrest him for disturbin' the public peace. 'Fore I get through with him he'll be glad to do worse things than marry you for the sake of gettin' free."

He grinned as he saw that Abrilla had by now got the girl in hand. She was no longer struggling; she couldn't, for the Mexican held her in a vise-like grip that would have spelled a broken limb for her had she fought him longer.

Lume let his insolent glance dwell lecherously upon her. "Pretty as a little red wagon," he complimented. "Even with your hair all mussed an' your shirt half torn from your back you're the best-lookin' hellcat Texas ever spawned!"

She eyed him in sullen defiance, a light in her glance that would have withered a lesser man than Lume. But Jarson Lume was used to women's tantrums and was not easily moved. There was no shame in him and his grinning lips were moist like a hungry wolf's.

"A foretaste of marital—" Lume broke off abruptly as the swinging doors banged inward. A breathless man burst into the place and stood there gulping while his round excited eyes took in the scene. Lume eyed him ominously, and his right hand slid inside his coat.

The man shrank back. "Don't shoot!" he panted. "I—ain't buttin' in! Shane's here!"

Lume tensed. "What's that?"

"Some fella—just brung 'im—in! He's claimin' the reward! Says he wants his money quick or he'll turn Shane loose!"

"Where is he?"

"They're both over to the Marshal's Office. Shane's tied onto his hoss."

"Hang onto the girl," Lume growled and, shoving the messenger out of his way, strode purposefully toward the door.

CHAPTER NINE

As Jarson Lume stepped out into the hot smash of the afternoon sun his right hand went to his black mustache in a caress that was the epitome of triumph. His cold eyes glowed with a savage satisfaction. Somehow, he reasoned, Sudden Shane had eluded the hurrying posse. But the result remained as pleasing for someone else had caught him. In Jarson Lume this drifter, Shane, had met his match!

Yes, the fruits of victory tasted sweet indeed to Jarson Lume as he strode along through the hock-deep dust on a tangent that would swiftly bring him to the Marshal's Office. He could see Shane slumped in his saddle, hands tied behind him, ankles lashed beneath his horse's belly, his shoulders sagging with the weariness of resignation. The mouth of Jarson Lume quirked maliciously as his glance took in the sight.

Even now Jarson Lume had commenced to gloat. Within his warped, malignant mind were visions of strange and cruel tortures which he proposed to swiftly administer to this man who had defied him, who had mocked him and with the bitter iron of fear made raw his soul. In ecstatic fancy he could hear Shane's sobbing cries and pleas for mercy. What had Shane against him to have treated him thus? Who was this drifting gun-slick? His agile mind swung down his past and found a number of disturbing possibilities. His lust for Shane's blood mounted.

The Marshal's Office at Tortilla Flat was an adobe addition to the peeled log building of the stage company. On a day like this it was an oven which even the flies shied away from. Just inside the door, astraddle of a chair, sat a slim wiry man whose abruptly grinning lips revealed a double row of bulging buck teeth.

Lume had made the acquaintance of this hombre at an earlier date and most emphatically did not like him. Sight of him now acted as a cold douche upon the rosy pictures in Lume's mind; they rocked, shivered and blacked out before a sudden premonition. What was this fellow doing here?

Passing the fettered Shane with hardly a glance Lume strode into the Marshal's Office and confronted the skinny outlander grimly. "Wasn't you told to get outa Tortilla Flat an' stay out?" he demanded.

"I sh'd say so," Bless Jones grinned. "But yer see I 'adn't any money an' figgered I'd ort ter get a stake ter-gether before I left. I seen one of yer reward posters describin' this hard-case hombre, Shane. Says I ter me,

'Jones, 'ere's yer charnce ter git a stake without much work, an' yer bloody well know it!' So I went out an' took 'im an' 'ere 'e is. W'ere's my money?"

Jarson Lume scowled at the angular speaker suspiciously. To his mind there was something altogether too glib about this fellow's tale. Yet he could not put his finger to anything especial.

"A pretty slick customer," he sneered.

"Blimey, yer said it—slick as they come!"

Lume fingered his tiny mustache thoughtfully. The man must be exceptionally handy with his pistol to effect the single-handed capture of this wildcat, Shane!

"Where'd you find Shane?"

"At 'is ranch. Does that make any diff'rence?"

"Well, no—but—"

"Never mind the buts. Wot I want is my money an' yer bloody well know it! Pay up or shut up!"

Lume's hand slid inside his coat as a dark wave of angry color flooded his cheeks. He was not accustomed to being spoken to in such a manner and resented it. This hard-case drifter was entirely too free with his chin music.

But he did not draw the gun his fingers sought. His reaching hand had hardly touched its handle when he found himself staring into the gaping orifice of a pistol conjured by Jones from the very air, apparently.

"Take it easy, Mister, unless yer yearnin' fer a harp an' halo!"

"I was getting you the money—" Jarson Lume began when Jones' strident laugh cut him off.

"Yus, I'll bet yer was!" Jones said, and prodded him

in the stomach with his pistol. "Get it now, an' don't get nothin' else less'n yer wantin' me ter knock a few stars in yer crown."

Lume produced his wallet and, under the watchful eye of his villainous-looking visitor, proceeded to count out a thousand dollars which Jones stowed carefully in the patched pocket of his shirt, while his right hand continued to prod Lume suggestively with the gun.

"Much obliged," he grinned. "I can see yer a real gent which knows the ol' saw about the laborer bein' worthy of 'is 'ire." Still keeping his gun on Lume, he backed away toward the door. But stopped short and tensed when a shot rang out from somewhere down the street, dry and diminutive in the vast immensity of the stifling afternoon.

"Wot's that?"

Lume too was scowling. "I don't know." His eyes mirrored a distinctly worried light which did not escape the wary orbs of Jones. "Untie Shane's feet and bring him in here. We'll put him in a cell."

Jones said, "Mebbe yer'd better put that gun yer totin' on the desk over there w'ere it won't be temptin' yer. An' be careful, Jarson, 'cause yer bloody well know I'd as lief shoot yer as look at yer."

After the gambler had deposited his weapon as bidden on the desk, he stared impatiently at Jones. "Well, get on about untyin' him. What are you waitin' for?"

Jones grinned slyly. "If there's any untyin' ter be done, yer the one that's goin' ter to do it." And he motioned with his gun significantly.

Lume's cold face was immobile as he strode past

Jones and out the door. But he could not keep the angry flame of vexation from his cheeks.

"Careful, now," Jones admonished with widening grin. "'E might kick yer in the chin. 'E's a vengeful hombre an' uncommon vicious in 'is 'abits."

Lume snorted and, bending, untied the buckskin thongs that lashed the prisoner's ankles beneath his horse's belly. But hardly had he done so when Shane's spurred heels smacked hard against the animal's ribs.

Lume jumped backward hurriedly in startled alarm as the horse rose to its hind legs snorting. The next instant its forehoofs came down smashingly and it was off in a cloud of dust that enveloped like a fog Jarson Lume's black-coated form.

The gambler's blazing eyes swung swiftly to Jones. That versatile individual was gaping after Shane's diminishing dust-screened figure with open mouth and bulging eyes.

Lume swore roundly. As though released from a spell by the gambler's abuse, Jones' drooping gun came up in a bursting arc of livid flame. The roaring reverberations smashed against the houses fringing the street on either side, but strangely Shane rode on with unabated speed—and that, despite the fact that his hands were lashed behind him!

"Blimey," ejaculated Jones, registering chagrin, "'e's got away!"

Lume, fists clenched, moved toward him ominously, his usually inscrutable face a mask of fury, his dark eyes gleaming balefully.

But, as though not noticing the gambler's advance,

Jones sprang hurriedly to his saddle. With swinging quirt and driving spurs Jones pounded after the vanishing Shane while Lume scorched the fetid air with mighty oaths.

A short distance out of town, screened from sight by a bend in the upward-climbing trail, Shane lounged in the saddle and waited for the pursuing Jones. When Jones reined his horse in beside him, Shane chuckled. "I'm allowin' that worked just like a charm."

Jones' lips curled derisively. "Blimey, it was like takin' candy from a kid! Lume swelled up like a poisoned pup w'en 'e seen yer dustin' outa town. Lumme! 'e's mad as a drunk squaw!"

"An' just as dangerous, I reckon," Shane said thoughtfully. Then he laughed. "Our little exploit ain't goin' to boost his stock a heap, I expect. He'll have to get us now to save his face."

"Won't 'e though?" Jones chuckled delightedly. "I wonder if 'e's 'eard the old one 'bout them as sups with the devil needin' long spoons?" Then, sobering, he added, "But just the same, between you, me, an' the gatepost, all that saved our bloody bacon was that stunt of yers, sendin' in that kid with that tale about yer bein' seen at Youngsburg. If that 'adn't pulled all 'is butcher-birds outa town, we'd be buzzard bait this minute!"

Shane nodded. "We better be rockin' along. You got that money?"

"'Ave I?" Jones displayed a toothy grin. "An' 'ow!"

Back in Tortilla Flat Jarson Lume was raging. Outwardly he was coldly saturnine, but deep inside his frozen-faced exterior he was an erupting volcano of destructive fury. He needed something to act as a safety valve to his turbulent emotions, and he had not long to seek to find the very thing he needed in the person of Pedro Abrilla, he who had been left to guard Lize Corbin.

When the boss of Tortilla Flat came striding savagely inside the Come-An'-Get-It he was all primed to force its owner to go through a marriage ceremony with him. He would show this bedeviling baggage who was boss in short order, he had told himself. He'd had enough of her tantrums and was all fed up. She would marry him before the sun went down or he would break her damned neck!

But when he got inside Lize Corbin's place his eyes sprang wide. He saw no sign of the girl but Pedro Abrilla was supporting himself against the counter with a shaking left hand, while his equally shaking right was clamped against his thigh as though to stop the bright red blood that was seeping steadily between his fingers. There was no gun in the holster on his belt; there was no weapon on the floor, either, other than Lize Corbin's discarded scatter-gun.

"Well, what's happened here?" asked Lume quietly, a grim note in his husky voice. "Where's the girl? How did you get shot? Why," he growled, with a touch of impatience that revealed a hint of the lashing bitterness and hatred that was gnawing away his habitual complacency, "don't you say something? Speak, by Gawd, or I'll shut you up for keeps!"

The Mexican lifted a grayish face that was filled with pain. What he read in Lume's blazing eyes drove him back against the counter, a look of dog-like pleading in his fearful glance.

"Senor! As the good God ees my weetness, I could not help eet! Thees hellcat snatch my peestol an' queek like a flash she fire! *Madre de Dios!* she ees one devil!"

Three swift steps brought Jarson Lume to a scowling stop before his wounded Myrmidon. In a brutal arc his right clenched hand slashed forward and stopped with a sodden thud against Abrilla's jaw. The luckless Mexican was flung off his feet as though struck by a flying beam. He lay where he fell, sprawled limply on his side with glazing eyes.

Jarson Lume dusted his knuckles and, with a final scowling glance about the place, shoved through the swinging doors and out into the dusty street.

Six hours later, with his back to the fireplace in his private office, he faced his men. They were a dusty, sullen-faced lot after their fruitless trip to distant Youngsburg chasing an elusive quarry who had never been there. He met their glowering looks with a stare that was hard as flint.

His voice was strongly alkaline, "I'm telling you for the last time that this damned leather-slappin' hellion has got to be rubbed out. I don't care how it's done, but I want it done quick. Each time I've sent a bunch against him he's outwitted 'em. What has happened to Kettle-Belly Dunn and Tularosa and the men who went with them, I don't know. I can't get a line on them. But I do know this; there hasn't a one of them turned up in this camp since!

"Something has got to be done sudden. I'll pay any two men of you fifteen hundred dollars apiece if this Shane disappears permanent inside the next twenty-four hours." His cold glance surveyed them grimly. "I'm askin' for volunteers."

No one spoke, none stepped forward or moved at all, in fact. The silence became a concrete thing through which men's breathing rasped uncomfortably. It grew long-drawn to the point of strangulation. Then Stone Latham's voice cut across it insolently:

"Why don't you take on the chore yourself an' save yore damned dinero?"

The air seemed to tighten up and chill. Yet no expression relieved the pale immobility of Jarson Lume's bloodless countenance. Neither by sniff nor scowl did he betray even a taint of thought or feeling. His instincts were locked behind the angles of his high-boned cheeks, behind the opaque hardness of his eyes and the straight-lipped line of his mouth.

He kept his glance on Latham fixedly, immovably, until Latham shifted his weight and sneered. And even then he held it there until the silence threatened once more to become insupportable. Then he said harshly:

"Since no one's volunteerin' for this chore I'm givin' it to Stone Latham and Lefty Hines. Twenty-four hours, I said. Remember. If the job ain't done inside that time you'll not get one damned penny. But you'll do the job just the same—or you'll answer to me."

No brag or bluster marked his tone, but the ominous threat his words contained was felt by all. Jarson

Lume was out for blood!

Sudden Shane, jogging along the winding trail that would take them to Keeler's Crossing, paid no further attention to his strange companion for some time. His thoughts persisted in dwelling upon the incomprehensible Lize Corbin. Not alone her clothes but her very personality was different from that of other women he had known. She was no wan, pale flower misplaced by mocking circumstances in this roaring mountain camp; she belonged here, yet there was something visibly wholesome about her that set her off from the others of her sex. Tomboyish, a creature of strong reactions, there was none the less something about her unutterably feminine and magnetic.

She contemplated life with eyes that, though rebellious, were unafraid. That something extremely odious was constantly threatening to leap from her past and overwhelm her was obvious. Yet she carried her head erect, her chin thrust bravely forward, defiant and unashamed.

Shane lashed himself with approbrium; he savagely resented her ability to dominate his thoughts. In moments of weakness he felt that he should have stopped by to see her while in Tortilla Flat; somehow he felt that she expected him to. But he hated himself for these moments of weakness; this girl was nothing to him—could never be anything to him. He had no wish for a more intimate relationship with her. He cursed the weak-kneed instance when first he had come to her defense, involving himself with Stone Latham and then with Lume, burdening himself with this succession of gunfights and dodgings that had followed in its wake.

He had come here for a purpose, and that purpose had nothing whatever to do with Lize Corbin. But instead of accomplishing his original design, all his time thus far had been occupied with turbulence occasioned by his stand with regard to this red-headed tomboy!

Hour after hour they rode northeast in silence. The dying sun sank lower, gilding the wilderness of towering crags and bastions about them with a veritable riot of shifting, glowing color. They seemed to be crawling toward the gates of heaven, such altitude they had attained. The air was crystal clear and filled with a piney tang, the dust and stifling heat left far below in that maze of canyons that now were filled with encroaching darkness.

Boulders, seemingly fashioned and dropped by mighty hands, strewed the bare escarpments that rose like bald-headed men about them, casting grotesque purple shadows that dappled the sunlit patches of greenish rock.

Higher and ever higher they climbed until at last they could look down upon the vast tumbled expanse of chaos that on maps is marked "Superstition Mountains." Great jagged divides, spiny hogbacks, desolate plateaus and mesas, long serpentine ridges—some sinister with dark masses of towering timber, others harsh and bleak in their ugly nakedness—lay spread about them like the toys of some weary giant. They could see Haystack Butte and Dutch Woman Butte, Methodist Mountain and Aztec Peak, their western-most reaches aglow like molten gold. Behind them Tortilla Mountain, Weaver's Needle and portions of the Apache Trail lay black and stark against the sun's last smile. To the southward Iron Mountain, Black Point and lesser crests rose in shimmering blues and lavenders, while ahead Granite Mountain, Nonesuch Rocks, Klondyke Mountain and the Apache Peaks seemed to frown upon their advance in sullen hate.

And now they were dipping down into the rising blackness of the night that hid all things in a swirling gloom. More slowly now than ever they went, each forward step a peril, a chance of falling untold feet to crash and rot on the unseen rocks below. It finally became so dark they dared not trust their ponies longer on this treacherous trail they followed, and they camped until the coming of the dawn.

In the first fierce light of the rising sun they resumed their way again, its dancing shafts throwing their elongated shadows before them and warming the frozen air.

They got their first view of Keeler's Crossing around seven-thirty, while still some distance off, and the sight dropped Jones' jaw.

"Albut's gorn!" he croaked.

Shane's lips pressed tight and grim. Alibi Albert Percival Smith was indeed gone, he saw. And gone was more, besides. Gone were the buildings of his ranch, reduced to a few charred posts and smouldering ashes!

CHAPTER TEN

THROUGH the stillness as Jarson Lume's voice trailed off, came the clattering thump of bootheels drumming out an approach. Lume's opaque eyes wheeled as the sounds came to a stop outside the door. Hard knuckles, beating roughly on its panels, awoke the echoes.

Jarson Lume growled softly, "Come in," and his hand slid inside his coat.

The door opened hesitantly and a little man came sidling in with a crab-like motion and stood blinking his close-set beady eyes in the yellow glow of the lamps. He ducked his head ingratiatingly the while his wary glance regarded the scowling men.

"Well, gents," he whined, "here I am."

Bronc Walders guffawed. "As if anybody give a damn!"

Lefty Hines heaved a grunt and bit another chew from his plug of tobacco.

Stone Latham said nothing, nor did he move in any way. He kept his eyes on Lume and his Indian cheeks were dark with resentment.

Lume said curtly, "Shut that door." And when the door was shut, "*Now,* we'll have your story—an' it better be good. Why ain't you with Kettle-Belly an' Tularosa?"

"Kettle-Belly's dead," whined Wimper, uneasily. "Tularosa killed 'im."

"What's that?" Lume snapped. "If you're lyin',

Wimper, I'll—"

"I ain't lyin', boss. You know I wouldn't lie to you. What I said is Gawd's truth, so help me—"

"What the hell do you know about Gawd?" Bronc Walders jeered.

Wimper paled and shrank back against the door as though wishing it were open. "It's truth, I'm tellin' you," he muttered desperately, well knowing the temper of these men. "Gawd's truth, so help me! Tularosa got big ideas—figured he'd break with you an' lead them paisanos in raids on his own an' hang onto what loot he took. Kettle-Belly mustn't of agreed with 'im, 'cause all of a sudden Tularosa pulled his knife an' let poor Kettle hev it to the hilt!"

"When'd this happen?" Lume scowled viciously.

"Same night we left here."

"Then where the hell you been ever since?" Bronc Walders snarled.

"I been with Tularosa. I couldn't git away. We been raidin' over round Globe. Yesterday mornin' he got the big idea there might be loot at the ol' ranch on Keeler's Crossin'. Figgered mebbe this Shane had that money—"

"I thought he'd spent that dinero he won here buyin' up the ranch," Lume interjected suspiciously.

"I dunno nothin' 'bout that," Wimper muttered. "I on'y know what he told the men. We rushed the place las' night. There was only one cuss there, a ugly lookin' jasper which Tularosa tortured in hopes he'd tell where Shane kep' his money. We left him down the pass a ways after we'd burned the buildin's."

"You mean to say that double-crossin' greaser burned that spread?" Stone Latham growled, roused at last from his silence by this angering news. "That's the place we hold the cattle while we're lettin' the brands heal over!"

"Sure, I know. Tularosa said that bein' we wasn't with Lume's crowd anymore it wasn't doin' us no good an' we better burn it so's to call a halt to your brand-switchin' ac—"

Lume cut him short with a ripped-out oath. "He *what!*"

"He said we better burn the ranch at Keeler's Crossin' 'cause it was the most important one you had, an' that if we gutted it right it would stop your boys from han-dlin' any more cattle till the buildin's an' c'rrals could be built up ag'in. Meantime, he proposed to grab that Bottle-A herd bein' held on Sunrise Mesa an' glut yore market. He figgers he can break you—"

Jarson Lume swore luridly through clenched teeth. There was a bloated look to his taut cheeks that was poisonous as he described in ghastly detail what he pro-posed to do with Tularosa when next their trails should cross.

When he stopped for lack of breath, Wimper said with a horrible smirk. "That won't be noways neces-sary, boss. I stopped his clock last night. Shoved my Bowie between his ribs, I did, an' cut my stick before them damn' paisanos found out what was up!"

The sun struck down on Keeler's Crossing like a brassy hammer, blistering the sand and dry-curled grass, heating the gritty wind until its breath was like the draft from a furnace. The sky shimmered like a sheet of tin.

Bless Jones, with one leg crooked about the saddle horn, regarded Shane gloomily. "Ain't this 'ell?" he sympathized. "Wot yer goin' ter do?" His glance played somberly across the charred remnants of the buildings they had spent two weeks repairing. "Skunks wot done this ort to be 'amstrung, by cripes!"

Shane grinned ruefully. "I been expectin' somethin' like this," he said. "I reckon it was too much to hope Lume wouldn't be payin' me back for buyin' this spread with money I took out of his Square Deal. He hasn't got no sense of humor."

"Yer bloody well know 'e ain't! Wot yer reckon they done with Albut?"

Shane's gray eyes clouded. He rasped his chin thoughtfully. "I wish I knew. I'm afraid—"

"Look!" Jones pointed excitedly up the trail leading down from the bluffs. "We're goin' ter 'ave comp'ny."

True enough; down the rocky trail a rider was coming slowly, carefully, lest a misstep spell disaster. The rider's clothes were worn and dusty and heavily-seamed with wrinkles; the shirt many-hued with patches. The rider was lithe and willowy, sure and graceful in the canted saddle, face concealed—save for a rounded chin—by the down-turned brim of a shabby hat.

Shane's eyes, as he watched this rider's progress, were narrowed thoughtfully. There was something familiar about the—

His thoughts were broken at this point by Bless

Jones' startled:

"Bless me! Hit's a gal!"

Shane swore beneath his breath as he recognized Lize Corbin, for she it was. And from Shane's viewpoint she could not have come at a more inopportune time. Right now a trip to Tortilla Flat was in order; a visit to even the score with Lume for the burning of these buildings. It was a thing he did not care to put off, for he was anxious to get in touch with Struthers and find out in what manner he could be of service to his dead brother's former pardner.

So it was he eyed the approaching girl with grumpy disfavor, though deep within him a voice cried out that he was glad to have her here. But he stifled its cry with savagery; he could not be burdened with a girl—he *would* not.

"Shane, y'u dang lunkhaid, h'are y'u?" She flashed him an eager smile, just as though her parting from Tortilla Flat had not been filled with turbulence and fraught with dire possibilities of shame.

She drew up nearby, sat lounging in her saddle while she regarded him expectantly. "Well," she managed, as the silence lengthened, "even if y'u ain't glad to see me, y'u might pretend y'u are. Yu look like I might hev poison ivy on me, or somethin'."

"Shucks, ma'am," Shane drawled, removing his hat—a gesture which was imitated by the watchful Jones. "I reckon I'm plumb glad to see you, but. . . ."

Her eyes flashed round, taking in the scattered heaps of ashes and the smoking, blackened posts. "This the spread y'u bought?" And at his nod, "Jarson's one fast worker, ain't he?"

Her glance swung back and searched his face. "But what?" her eyes were on his squarely.

"But—" Shane shifted uncomfortably, finding his saddle unusually hard. "But . . . Well, you see, ma'am, right now I got a heap to do an'—" he floundered hopelessly beneath her level regard, his sun-darkened cheeks showing his embarrassment. "I—I—"

Her head went up, like that of a spirited pony. Scorn flashed from the stormy eyes that stabbed his conscience. Her mouth became a white and twisted line.

"Why lie? I reckon y'u have heard them things that's bein' said about me. Oh, I know what that lousy town is sayin'! I guess y'u are scared y'u'll get *contaminated!* Well, y'u needn't to worry—I'll keep away!" And, with a choked little sob, she whirled her horse and roweled across the muddy creek and into the trail to Globe.

"Here—wait!" Shane called, but without avail.

"Blimey!" Jones said. "Yer done it now!"

When Lize Corbin raced away from Keeler's Crossing, she was shaking with a fury she had never known before; the hatred and resentment she had felt for the man who had betrayed her and then ignominiously cast her aside for a newer flame was as nothing to the storm aroused in her by Shane.

She drove her horse with quirt and spur, caring not where she went so long as it was away. She rode with a red fog before her eyes and a terrible ringing in her ears. Her heart beat against her breast with a tumult that seemed certain to loosen it from her body, and her breathing came in panting sobs.

Miles sped beneath the pony's hoofs like paces, yet still she urged him on. The drive of the whistling wind, the fierce clattering pound of hoofs and headlong careening movement blent well with the storm within her and in some small measure seemed to ease her tortured spirit.

That Shane, of all men, should have treated her thus! Had he driven a knife in her heart and twisted, he could not have hurt her more. What a horrible thing to find oneself madly in love with a man who valued one's regard so lightly! With a man who cared no whit whether one were near or miles away! With a man who appeared to *prefer* one somewhere else!

It was hateful, contemptible, *unbearable!*

But it was true!

She lashed her spirit raw with bitter, endless thoughts of Shane until at last exhausted, her passion consumed in its own white flame, she brought her lathered pony to a halt.

She cast a heedful glance about. Rimrock seemed to hem her in from all directions save ahead. Ahead the trail rose twisting through a veritable maze of boulders; boulders small, toadlike and ugly; boulders towering tall and mighty; reddish boulders squatted precariously and sinister in the sand and clacking rattle-weed.

This looked like the trail to Globe, she thought, and shuddered to think she'd ridden its tortuous path in such abandon. Her red lips quivered and tears fell unchecked upon her cheeks.

But presently her sobbing ceased, "Bawlin' like a spoiled brat!" she upbraided herself, and added, "Lize Corbin, yo' a gosh-blamed fool!"

She smiled a little at that, a wan pathetic smiling of the lips. "Sure is lucky none of them lunkhaids back at the Flat is watchin' me now. I reckon they'd git a big kick outa seein' Dry-Camp Corbin's tomboy snifflin'." She shook her head disgustedly. "I must be gittin' soft!"

She peered beneath a shading hand at the trail ahead. After all, it did not greatly matter where she went as long as never again her eyes should fall on Shane, or Lume, or Latham. She would never return to Tortilla Flat where Lume could have his will with her; she must hide herself some place beyond his reach!

With the thought she straightened bravely in the saddle; with her knees she urged her tired pony on. Perhaps she dare not linger in Globe, but Globe would do for now—it must.

She rode with shoulders drooped dejectedly. What was the use of running away? Lume would run her down and bring her back; she knew it. There was no escaping him. She recalled that others had tried before. And, anyway, what did it matter? Nothing seemed to matter now. . . .

The stopping of her pony roused her from the gloomy, forlorn mutations of her thoughts. She looked up to find the trail a narrow ribbon between two towering walls of greenish, frowning rock. A horseman blocked her path, sat lounging comfortably with one knee crooked about his silvered saddle horn. A cigarro depended limply from his gloating lips, its upward-spiralling smoke diffusing against the braided brim of his huge, chin-strapped sombrero. There was a light in his squinting eyes she did not like.

He was a big, huge mountain of a man, she saw. Sleek and swarthy, with black bushy brows overhanging piercing dark eyes that held just now a feline glitter as he found her glance upon him. His shirt was silk and lavender, there were flowers embroidered on his waistcoat that partly covered it, and about his middle was tied a bright red sash. His wine-colored velvet trousers had slashed bottoms, the seams alive with gleaming silver. White teeth abruptly flashed in the burnished copper of his face.

"Buenas dias, senorita," he offered languidly, and doffed his huge sombrero with a calculated flourish.

"What do y'u want?"

"Ah, but did I say that I weeshed anytheeng?"

"Then turn yo' hoss an' let me pass," there was no compromise in Lize Corbin's level tone. She was badly scared by the things to be read in his gloating eyes, but she would not let him know it.

"The day ees too warm for such hurry, senorita. Your caballo, he needs the rest. I myself, Manuel Tularosa, shall find eet plaisant to beguile your tedious hours."

"Move pronto, hombre, or I'll let y'u hev it!" Lize Corbin's whip rose threateningly. She knew that name and quailed within for tales of Tularosa, and his way with women, had traveled far. "Move, I say!"

Tularosa's grin was mocking. "My," he said, and "My!"

She swung her quirt and he took it on his arm and

before she could pull it back, with a swift jerk he snatched it from her, wrenching her wrist painfully in the act. "Tularosa shall pull your fangs, leetle hellcat," and he threw the whip behind him.

She shrank from his leering face and made to whirl her horse. But he was too swift for her. Like a snake his arm shot out and grasped her pony's reins.

"Not so fas', my dove," he taunted, slipping from his saddle sinuously.

The next she knew she was in his arms, struggling desperately but ineffectually. There was a great roaring in her ears, a blackness before her eyes. But she could feel. . . .

She could feel his heavy breathing on her face, and she could feel his supple muscles contracting as he crushed her to him with one great arm. She could feel the clumsy pawing of his hand.

How long this horror continued she could not tell, but suddenly she almost swooned for joy when a cold, familiar drawl said:

"Hist 'em, polecat!"

Tularosa's crushing arm fell loose and she staggered back to see Shane sitting his horse six feet away, his features stiff as some mask chopped out of wood.

Tularosa crouched like some great puma, glaring at the sudden apparition through bloodshot, narrowed eyes. His mouth was twisted in an ugly sneer and a muscle jerked spasmodically in his left cheek.

Shane swung lithely from the saddle. Lize watched him with cheeks that were deathly white, her former anger forgotten in the thralling interest of the moment.

Her personality reached strongly across the stillness, pulling at her heartstrings.

She watched him swing forward a pace or two, his cat-like step hinting at a smooth coordination of mind and muscle that very shortly might prove deadly. She had a three-quarters view of his countenance. It was hard and colorless and taut; only his eyes seemed alive. They were heated with a smouldering, wanton flame.

She did not see his lips move but the cold, soft drawl of his words brought her a thrill of involuntary admiration:

"Mister, I reckon you thought this was your opportunity. I allow you was figurin' to make a little hay while the sun was shinin', so to speak. I'm sort of wonderin' if you are still inclined thataway?"

Tularosa sneered, white teeth flashing wolf-like in his copper face. His right arm stiffened perceptibly, bent above his holstered gun, his fingers spread in a claw-like droop. Lize could see the malignant hate and menace that glowered from his dark, deep-socketed eyes.

"Mister, I'm allowin' I'm goin' to kill you," Shane said harshly. And now to Lize the full intensity of his awful rage became apparent. There was an inexorable compression to his straight thin-lipped mouth that told of deadly purpose; his blazing eyes held smoking fury.

"Draw, you polecat—*draw!*"

For an instant there was entire silence in the canyon. Then thunderous echoes split it wide as Tularosa's hand swooped down and up. She could hear the whine of his hurried lead. Then Shane shot coldly from the hip—just once. Dust jumped from Tularosa's vest. She saw a cold grin cross Shane's face as the Mexican clutched at his chest and, staggering, crumpled backward in the dust.

CHAPTER ELEVEN

SHANE looked at Lize and tried to say something but no words would come. He wanted to put his arms round her and apologize for his lack of enthusiasm when she had come to him at Keeler's Crossing. Instead, he sheathed his gun and built a smoke with slightly trembling hands. When he had it going and could no longer find an excuse in the business of its manufacture, he said gravely,

"I reckon we better be ridin', ma'am."

Then he looked at her again. "Good Lord, Lize!" he blurted, and was beside her in an instant, and she was clinging to him, her wet face hid against his chest while relieving sobs shook her slender body.

Even after they had mounted, and he had settled in his saddle, Shane's blood still throbbed to her kisses. Hungrily his shining eyes fed on the soft pale oval of her face, on her fiery hair and scarlet lips, and on the new, shy wonder in her eyes. He was amazed that he could not control the tremble of his body as he covertly studied her while they turned their horses back toward Keeler's Crossing. What mattered the cost, what mattered his mission, if he could secure this sweet rare loveliness for his own?

Passion he had not known that he possessed was in his blood; excitement, like a potent wine, pulsed through his veins. They rode in silence for a time while Shane strove mightily to bring some sort of coherent order out of the wild, ecstatic turmoil in his mind.

At last succeeding, he fell to meditating upon the predicament into which his new-found emotion for this girl was placing him. Obe Struthers had written his brother Jeff for help. Shane had taken up the burden out of reverence to Jeff's memory. But, so far, he had not managed to even talk with Struthers, though already he had been in Struthers' neighborhood for several weeks. *Now,* his new relationship to Lize was going to make this more difficult than ever. For how was he to go running risks for Struthers without a place to leave the girl? And he had no place. Even the doubtful security of the Keeler's Crossing ranch was no longer available!

He frowned a little in his intentness to find a solution.

Lize, with flushed cheeks and a touch of pride in her lifted chin, chose that moment to look at him. A little of the fire went out of her eyes at sight of his frown and she watched him anxiously.

But Shane, all unaware, continued wrestling with his problems, and his frown grew deeper, darker.

He could leave her, he was thinking, with Bless Jones. But where could he leave Bless Jones? The only answer seemed to be for the three of them to seek Obe Struthers out and if there was work for Shane to do, then let Struthers himself provide a safe retreat for Lize until Shane's work was finished.

That settled with himself, Shane relaxed a little and gave his thoughts to this ranch that he had purchased with money wrung from Lume's Square Deal. Who had burned his buildings? Lume? Or some of Lume's cohorts? But if so, why? And why had they thought fit to take Alibi Smith with them, unless they planned to use him for a hostage? And then, a hostage for what? Ransom? It seemed unlikely, at best.

His revolving thoughts turned to the burly Mexican he had bested. He felt no regret for killing that brute. Indeed, he felt a kind of savage satisfaction. Who had the fellow been? With slight curiosity he asked, more for the sake of making conversation than for any other reason.

"That . . . that *hombre;* who was he? Would you be knowin', ma'am?"

A look of loathing crossed the girl's flushed face. "Tularosa," she answered with repugnance. "A leader of hoss thieves, cattle rustlers, and cutthroats. I think he was connected with Jarson Lume." She regarded him curiously as he frowned. "Why?"

"I'm sort of tryin' to connect him up with things. Any of that tough bunch in town been botherin' you again?"

She hesitated and the flush deepened perceptibly in her cheeks. She caught the narrowing of his eyes and said, "Jarson was figurin' to marry me, yesterday. He—"

She broke off with a subtly pleasant, tingling as she saw his face grow dark.

Shane growled, "The orn'ry pup! I reckon he needs a talkin' to. . . . An' I'm allowin' he's due to get one. Wanted to marry you, did he? When was this?"

"Yesterday afternoon. He thinks Dry-Camp Corbin passed me on the location of his mine. Seems like he'd

120

given up his schemes fo' gettin' me to talk. I reckon he figured he'd marry me so's if the mine ever turned up he'd be in a position to grab it."

"Did—?" Shane began. But Lize cut him short with a scornful laugh.

"No, I sloped. He was all set an' sendin' fo' the preacher when some fella came bulgin' in a-yowlin' that some other gent had ridden in with y'u a pris'ner an' was shoutin' fo' his money. Lume must be right anxious to collect yo' scalp, I reckon, 'cause he went bangin' out the doah like the devil beatin' tan bark! I sure was scared fo' a minute, but I knowed y'u'd make the riffle so I cut my stick an' here I am."

"I reckon Jarson Lume," Shane growled, "would eat off the same plate with a snake."

Her blue eyes twinkled fleetingly. "He's a pow'ful orn'ry man." Resentment obscured the twinkle the next moment and she added huskily, "There's others jest as bad."

"I reckon you're thinkin' of Stone Latham, ma'am. An' I'm allowin' he's in need of gentlin', too. I'm figurin—" he broke off, struck by the peculiar expression in her eyes. "Why, what's the matter, Lize?" His voice was anxious.

"Nothing!" She managed a shaky laugh; said lamely, "I was jest thinkin'." But she did not confide what her thoughts had been about. Instead she changed the subject. "Who was that puncher I seen y'u with at Keeler's Crossin'?"

"Name's Bless Jones. Horace, his father called him, but he allows he ain't right partial to that handle." His lips quirked as at some humorous memory. "Tells me he come from England. He's folks over there, I reckon. Said his father was the earl of somethin'-or-other—Dickhouse, I believe he said. Anyhow, he's some fast on the trigger. I hired him an' another gent to work my spread. I reckon since last night what I need most is carpenters," he grinned ruefully.

Prolonged inactivity was awakening spluttering fires of impatience and discontent among the rank and file of Lume's renegade supporters. They wanted gold to spend in gambling and more gold to throw away on the wenches of the camp. To get this so-necessary gold they must stage another robbery or stick up another stage or move their waiting cattle. Lume did not want any more robberies just now; things were shaping up, he said. To stick up a stage right now would be fruitless and even dangerous, for Lume had taken over the last large independent mine and such gold as was being shipped belonged to him. As for moving the cattle—impossible. Tularosa had burned the big corrals at Keeler's Crossing where of old it had been customary to hold the critters while altered brands scabbed over and still other brands were made through a wet blanket, and the next ranch in their owlhoot string was a long hard drive that must, in part, be pushed under the very noses of outraged authority.

But inactivity was bad, as Bronc Walders pointed out to Lume a short time after Hines and Latham had left on their lethal mission to Shane. Like the insidious growth of some unseen cancer it was undermining

Lume's influence and dominance. Bronc Walders said as much.

"Look," he pointed out. "You better be givin' these wolves of yores somethin' to occupy their hands. When scum like them gets to usin' their hatracks, all hell is due to come apart!"

Lume grinned like a sleek black cat. "They're goin' to have their han's full pronto. Wimper," he faced the pock-marked whiner with an abruptness that shrank the little man back against the wall, "when this meetin' breaks up you corral all the loose saddle bums that's loafin' round here an' start shovin' them cattle we got at Horse Mesa on towards our Iron Mountain spread—"

"You can't do that!" Shoshone Mell jerked out. "No men can shove that bunch of wall-eyed brutes over that kinda country in a jump as long as—"

"I want them cattle started for Iron Mountain before mornin'!" Lume's voice contained no compromise. "An' by Gawd, Wimper, that scum of yours better get 'em there." There was something in Lume's eyes as he said the last that set the pock-faced man a-shiver. Lume's glance then whipped to Mell.

"I'm wanting that Corbin dame, Mell. You an' Alder bring her in."

Men rasped his unshaven jaw. "I ain't keen," he muttered hesitantly, "on monkeyin' with no damn skirt. Better pick someone else—"

"I'm pickin' *you*, Mell; you an' Birch Alder," Lume's voice was dangerously soft. "But I ain't askin' you to run such risk for nothing. There's two grand apiece in it for you if you can cut it. An',," he added ominously, "you better cut it."

Mell shrugged philosophically and took up some slack in his belt.

"Uh-huh," he said.

Bronc Walders, watching, grinned behind his lips.

Lume looked at Alder curiously, calculation in his glance. "Got any notion where to look?"

Alder nodded. He said bruskly, "I'm allowin' we have. Mebbe you ain't noticed it but that dame's a heap sweet on this Shane hairpin. Looks like aces to kings she'll be headin' for Keeler's Crossin'. I figger we'll amble over thataway a piece."

Bronc Walders' lips drew down; his eyes clouded up.

When Alder and his crony got up to leave several moments later, Bronc Walders too arose. He was following them to the door when Lume said,

"Wait a minute, Bronc. I got a little somethin' I'd like to be talkin' over with you."

Walders turned and his eyes slid over Wimper who grinned ingratiatingly.

Walders said, "You ain't figurin' to habla 'bout anythin' private with that scissors-bill hangin' round, are you?"

Lume looked at Wimper. "Clear out, Wimper. I'll see you in the mornin'."

"Heck, I—" Wimper broke off short and scuttled for the door as Lume's cold glance started storming up. Lume sneered when the door slammed shut behind him. "Minds just like a dog."

"I wouldn't have a squirt like him around," Walders

124

growled. "That little shrimp would sell his gran'mother down the river if he figured she'd bring a profit!"

Lume grinned. "You're gettin' jittery. Hell, I got Wimper right under my thumb. He's almost scared to breathe aroun' me."

Walders grunted. "Even a rat will bite." He looked at Lume inquiringly. "What was you wantin' to see me about?"

"I got some . . ." Letting his voice trail off, Lume reached inside his coat.

Something in his eyes must have given his intention away for Walders' hand dove hipward frantically—too late!

Flame lanced wickedly from Lume's reappearing hand. Rocking, roaring reverberations filled the room and set the lamplight flaring. Hot blood streamed down Bronc Walders' forehead and into his glazing eyes. He staggered blindly, lips parting grotesquely as he swayed and dropped. His hat fell off and rolled across the floor and Jarson Lume laughed mockingly as he stood above him, his smoking pistol still in hand.

Someone was pounding on the door but Lume paid no heed.

"So Wimper'll double-cross me, eh?" he sneered, derision in his glance. "Well, you blasted ranger spy, I'm damned sure *you* won't write Shane no more notes!"

"When Stone Latham finds out what Lume is up to there'll be hell a-poppin' sure!" Birch Alder said to Mell as they left the Square Deal and stood beside the hitch rack untying their horses' reins. "D'you reckon

Lume knows what he's doin'?"

"If he don't, it's sure enough high time he was findin' out," Mell grinned. "He may be cock-o'-the-walk in this man's camp, but Stone Latham is no safe man to fool with. You reckon that lousy Wimper really shoved a knife in Tularosa? Sounds mighty thin to me."

"Me, too," Alder concurred, swinging into the saddle. "Yuh know, Shoshone, I ain't real keen on this chore Lume has dished us out. I'd like it a heap better, I'm allowin', ef Latham wasn't mixed up in it. He'll be after somebody's scalp damn sure!"

"Yeah, I reckon. But two grand is two grand, no matter where you spend it. I ain't seen that much money in a coon's age."

"We ain't seen it *yet,* neither," Birch Alder reminded grimly. "I wouldn't put it past Lume to have us grab the dame an' then hightail it without payin' off."

"He better not look like it," growled Shoshone Mell. "Let's git goin'."

"What we goin' to do if the dame's with Shane?"

"Hang round outa sight till Shane has business elsewhere. Hell, he can't wet-nurse her like a yearlin' calf! He's gotta leave 'er sometime. When he does is when we act. Dig spurs an' let's git started. I wanta git my fingers on that dinero."

Stone Latham and Lefty Hines were half way to Keeler's Crossing when Latham abruptly pulled in his horse. "You better camp here till mornin'," he told his companion. "Too damn dark to tackle the rest of the way tonight. Don't build no fire or—"

126

"What the hell?" growled Hines. "Ain't you goin' to be here?"

"Not sure, yet. I got a little matter to attend over round Weaver's Needle. If I can make it in time I'll join you."

"You don't think I'm figgerin' to tackle Shane by myself, do you?"

Latham sneered. "Hell, you can lay back of some boulder an' pot him off, can't you?"

"Not by myself, I can't! I got too much respect for my hide," Hines answered resentfully. "By cripes, I'm allowin' I'll wait right here till you git back."

"Don't be a fool. You—"

"I'd be a fool all right if I was to go solo after that damn' leather-slapper!"

Latham regarded his companion thoughtfully in the starlight. He cleared his throat once or twice. Finally he remarked, "There ain't really any reason why we should jump this Shane, you know."

Hines started. After a moment's silence, "I guess you're right," he said. "What you got in mind?"

"It might not be a bad idea if we pulled out. Lume's headin' for the rocks. I got a feelin' the minute I clapped eyes on Shane that Jarson's number was damn-well up. I'm gettin' plumb fed up on his domineerin' ways, anyhow. What say we cut our stick? Lume's figurin' to ship out some dust tomorrow night. We might stop the stage an' make a haul." He looked at Hines craftily.

Hines shrugged. "Well, that suits me," he said. "But what about yore woman?"

A scowl crossed Latham's features and his high-boned cheeks grew dark. "What was that remark?"

Hines read a warning in that soft-toned purr. "I said," he muttered hastily, "that I'd be plumb proud to help you stop the stage."

Stone Latham grunted and relaxed. "A loose jaw," he spoke reminiscently, "has helped many a gent into a quiet bunk under Boot Hill's weeds." He began pulling the saddle from his horse. "The fella that's learned to hobble his tongue is the gent who's goin' to live long enough to be tellin' boogery tales to his gran'children. Let's rest these nags a spell."

"Tomorrow," Shane said to Jones, after Lize Corbin had turned in between her blankets and he and Jones sat smoking beside the campfire, "we're headin' for Tortilla Flat. I got to find a fella named Struthers who owns a mine."

When Shane had returned to Keeler's Crossing a couple of hours before, Jones had exhibited no surprise at seeing the girl accompanying him. Now he ventured, hesitantly, "What you figgerin' ter do with the calico?" and he jerked his thumb toward where Lize lay. "Goin' ter take 'er along?"

"Have to," Shane admitted. "No place here to leave her. I'm goin' to put it up to Struthers to find a place for her till I get through with a few chores I got mapped out."

"If them chores 'as got anything ter do with that bloke, Lume, I'd admire ter 'ave a part in 'em," he growled. "I owe that bloke a couple."

Shane grinned. "I'm allowin' that Jarson Lume will

128

figure in them some prominent. I expect he's been takin' all the profit out of Struthers' mine an' Struthers is aimin' to have me see what can be done. We'll have to keep our eyes skinned when we get to town. Some of Lume's hired polecats'll prob'ly have their guns oiled up for us."

"Don't yer know it!" Bless Jones grinned.

"I wish," Shane said soberly, "I knew who sent us that warnin' the other day. I'd hate mighty much to find I'd perforated him by mistake, along with Lume an' the rest of them renegades."

He sighed. "Well, let's turn in so's we can get an early start."

CHAPTER TWELVE

MORNING has a way of coming swiftly on the desert; a burst of orange flame sears the rim of the world and night is changed to day. But in the mountains it is different.

A pale wan light comes crawling insidiously across the earth, and the darkness slowly scatters on the heights while the stars and moon grow dim. The chill of daybreak snaps into the air and the farflung canyons' depths loom gray and desolate among the tumbled chaos of upthrust crag and bastion. Slowly the eastern skyline seems to crack and great red jagged streaks leak through its misty veil. Then the veil itself dissolves before this warming influence and the heavens become a brilliant, flawless blue through which the sun's fiery ball slowly rises, cloaking each towering spire and rocky escarpment in robes of shimmering gold.

And so it was on this morning as Shane and Jones and Lize Corbin rode in leisurely silence toward distant Tortilla Flat. Shane had intended going to the Flat three days ago, as he had confided to Jones that night beside the campfire. But one thing and another had cropped up to change his mind and cause him to postpone the trip. One of these things was the presence of Lize Corbin.

Each passing hour he felt more strongly drawn to the girl. Why? He could not have told. He found something strangely alluring in the poise of her flaming head and in certain of her mannerisms. He loved the expressive Latin way in which she shrugged her shapely shoulders. He counted the time well spent when he watched the sunlight glinting through the copper of her hair and he took a personal pleasure in observing the varying shades of blue that flashed from her level eyes.

Sometimes he detected surprise in the glance she threw him when he did little things he knew would please her, and there were occasions when there were gleams of jealousy in her gaze though he had been unable to figure exactly why.

That she was a creature of impulse, he understood. But a flame of loyalty, he had discovered, burned strong and high within her. And he recognized, as in himself, that in her there was a stubborn streak that would ever refuse to consider the chance of defeat for anything she set out to do. It must have come as an inheritance from her dad, old Dry-Camp Corbin.

When walking, she had a clean-limbed stride that fascinated, and she could ride as well as any man. She made a mighty attractive picture as she rode along ahead of him with the sunlight striking down across her hair. He reflected that soon she would have to put on her wide-brimmed hat, for the morning was rapidly growing hot. He sighed, and squinted out across the country spread about them.

The surface of this land was slashed and broken by the deep purple gashes of ravines and gullies and canyons which seemed to alternate in some crazy, incomprehensible manner with timbered ridges, long shaley hogbacks and flat-topped buttes and mesas that already lay shimmering in distorting stratas of heat. This writhing haze traced distant mountains in dim blue etchings across the buckling skylines and even made a few more-favored ones appear deceptively near.

As the morning advanced the hot smash of the brassy sun beat down upon the thirsty earth with increased venom. The overheated air grew stifling; filled with tiny dust particles that irritated dry throats and nostrils as a red rag does a bull and reddened the rims of smarting eyes.

Then suddenly Bless Jones pulled rein where he rode in the lead. He sat motionless in the saddle scanning dead ahead from beneath a shading hand. When Shane and the girl had joined him, he growled, "Wot yer make of that? Looks like dust ter me—mebbe cattle, or mebbe 'orses."

Shane, following the direction indexed by Jones' outthrust pointing hand, saw a boulder-rimmed ugly gash leading into a valley some seven or eight miles off.

Above the gash drifted a lazy ephemeral cloud which he knew for dust.

"You're right, Bless," he admitted. "That *is* dust. Somebody's shovin' cattle into that valley, looks like. Now I'm wonderin' why they'd be wantin' to do that? I'd say that valley wouldn't graze more'n three scrawny critters for half a day."

"Yer bloody well knows it," Jones affirmed.

"Rustlers!" Lize Corbin said with curling lips. "Some of Jarson Lume's long-loopers. I'm bettin' y'u bedded down on one of Jarson's relay spreads!"

"Relay spreads?" Shane looked puzzled. "What you mean, ma'am? I didn't know Lume was in the cattle business."

"Well, he handles critters off an' on. Mostly other folks' critters, I reckon. They steal 'em one place, so the rumor goes, an' drift them a few at a time down a chain of small spreads until they emerge in some other state under a diff'rent brand—a brand that's good as gold."

"I still don't see—"

"Look!" the girl exclaimed. "If y'u happened to buy a ranch that was in the middle of his string, for instance, he'd be stuck with the cattle he had at the other end, wouldn't he? Well, then, he'd have to get y'u out; one way'd be burnin'. Somebody burned yo' place, didn't they?"

"Yer damn well shoutin'!" growled Jones, and spat. "Wot's more, they done poor Albut in!"

Lize looked questioningly at Jones. Shane said, "He means Alibi Smith, a fella I hired who's disappeared."

"Oh!" her face whitened. She laid a hand on Shane's

arm. "I'm so sorry," she said impulsively. "Won't anyone ever stop him? Him and the men under him have practically made the boneyard at Tortilla Flat—"

"They may be decoratin' it themselves before this thing is finished," Shane cut in grimly. "Do you know an ol' codger called Obe Struthers—"

"The mining man?"

Shane nodded.

"I've heard of him. He used to own the Copper King—"

"*Used* to own?" Shane's eyebrows raised. "Don't he own it no more?"

Lize Corbin's eyes darkened swiftly; her mouth was tight and white when she answered.

"No—he sold out to Jarson Lume."

The muscles tightened along Shane's clenched jaw. "I thought," he said slowly, "that the Copper King was a pretty good thing."

"It was dang good, I reckon," Lize told him. "Jarson Lume don't never bother acquirin' mines what ain't no account."

Shane's cheeks paled with anger. To him it seemed plain that pressure—considerable pressure—must have been brought to bear on Struthers to effect this sudden sale.

"Where's Struthers now?"

"I heard he was hangin' out at the Miner's Rest. Someone said he was figgerin' to locate another bonanza. He'll be a fool if he does, 'cause Lume'll gobble it jest like he done the Copper King an' a whole passel of other mines in these here mountains."

"It's just possible, I'm allowin'," Shane drawled heavily, "that Lume'll be coughin' up these mines again. A fella can't never tell. Stranger things has happened." His eyes swept over the distant valley. "Cattle, all right," he said. "Some consid'rable. They're millin'—see? Them punchers is figurin' to rest 'em."

He looked appraisingly at Jones. "I'm wonderin' if you'd like to pay 'em a visit, Bless?"

Jones grinned felinely. "Yer sure said somethin' that time."

"Got plenty cartridges?"

Lize looked from Shane to Jones. Then she grabbed Shane's arm. "Don't do it, Sudden!" Her cheeks were paling in swift alarm. "Look—y'u couldn't cut it! There's six riders with them cow-critters. Six to two! Y'u wouldn't stand a chance!"

Shane smiled mirthlessly. "We wouldn't figure on stackin' up against them fellas. There's other ways a couple of smart hairpins could keep them steers from leavin' this country. How about it, Bless?"

"Yer on!" Jones said, and winked. "Might give 'em a bit of their own, wot?"

The western sky glowed like molten copper as the sun slid down behind the purple mountain crests and flung their elongated shadows obliquely out across the valley. There was more grass here than Shane had thought, but there was none too much and Wimper, as he sat his saddle gazing out across the restless cattle, was feeling boogery. It might be wiser, he opined, to shove them on a bit and risk the chance of scanter forage than to remain in this rimrocked hole where the cattle were plainly uneasy.

Yet it was getting late in the afternoon and he did not relish the thought of pushing these lowing brutes across this treacherous terrain once night fell. The valley's lack of water was the factor which finally decided him. He beckoned a circling rider.

When the fellow rode up, Wimper said, "Shove 'em on. We'll try for a better place. This hole's too blasted dry an' hot. Come night, these critters'll be in a mood to bolt if a cricket creaks. Get 'em rollin', Ed."

The puncher scowled. "We might have to bed 'em down in a worser place," he objected.

Wimper went ugly and his hand dropped suggestively to his hip. "Who's roddin' this drive?" his voice held no sign of its usual whine. His pock-marked face flamed darkly. "You go pass the word along that we're movin'—now!"

The rider muttered, but cantered off.

Soon the moving cattle were rolling up a stifling cloud of dust as they streamed eastward from the valley, swinging down a wide stone-carpeted draw. This soon widened to such an extent that Wimper felt justified in hoping it might broaden into another valley. A bigger one perhaps, with grass.

An hour later his hope came true. The forward-dancing shadows of the bawling herd reached out across an undulating plain. Waving grasses that reached knee-high attested to the presence of water. "Springs, most likely," Wimper growled to one of his companions. "Start 'em millin', Joe."

Joe and the others did their work well and two hours later, having detailed three men to circle riding, Wimper returned to the tiny campfire the cook had been sweating over and had supper with the rest. At nine-thirty he wrapped himself up in his blanket and lay down with his booted feet to the fire.

Sometime in the night Wimper sat bolt upright, staring into the dark. The fire was reduced to a heap of glowing embers. There was no moon and only a few faint stars were visible in the leaden vault of heaven. Miles away a lightning flash threw a pale illumination and was gone. An unknown fear held Wimper motionless.

A breath of cooler air brushed his taunted cheeks. In the darkness around him he could hear the swishing of the long grasses in the gathering wind. Scattered drops of rain struck down. Ashes swirled about the embers of the campfire. Wimper shivered.

A pulse of nervous excitement beat against his throat. Yards away his attention was caught and held; his eyes dilated. Something was stirring soundlessly in that yonder gloom. Its movements held the stealth of a stalking cat—a mountain cat. A fear, swift and searing, brought him to his feet with a muttered oath.

His bulging eyes clung fascinated to that dim-seen, swift-flitting shadow in the lesser darkness of the mid-night gloom. There came a sound like the crunch of booted feet on gravel. The deep bronze of Wimper's cheeks gave place to a sickly pallor. Throat parched with fear he yanked his gun.

But he did not fire. Thunder rumbled hollowly in the

136

distance on the heels of another lightning flash. Wimper held his lean-muscled little body moveless; only the close-set restless eyes stabbing here, there, and all about gave hint of the tension under which he labored. Then suddenly—

"Christ!" he cried.

Off there in the night, northeastward, a point of light was flickering, growing, red against the murk. And even as Wimper stared another tiny flame licked up from farther to the north and gathered headway rapidly, fanned by the wind sweeping through the swishing grasses.

With twitching body and the desperation of a trapped rat Wimper scuttled for his horse, colliding with another form which—springing from its blankets—seemed motivated by the same idea.

Wimper cursed with lurid fury as fear spurred him to his feet. Both men reached their horses simultaneously; jerked the saddle cinches tight and flung themselves aboard.

Wimper flung one hurried look backward across his shoulder. "Roll yore tail, boy! That fire'll be a ragin' fury inside the next two minutes!"

The puncher, too, looked rearward. The flames were gaining headway fast; great fiery tongues were showing above a dense black rolling cloud of smoke that was pouring toward the bedded herd.

"What about the cattle?"

"To hell with the blasted cattle!" Wimper shouted, and used his spurs with desperation, for well he knew that once those cattle tore loose all the cowboys in the world could never stop their headlong rush within a distance of several miles—and that fire would drive them the very way that he, too, was forced to head.

It was not a thought one cared to linger on, and Wimper was doing no lingering.

His big roan ran for all it was worth, but now above its pounding hoofs Wimper could hear the frightened bawling of the cattle as they came lumbering to their feet. Somewhere not far behind him a frenzied steer let out a defiant challenge that set the herd in motion.

Again Wimper flashed a look behind. Three of his men were strung out there on pounding ponies and behind them like the fantastic background of some melodramatic painting plunged the bawling herd, tails up, a churning indistinct bellowing mass of frenzied beef.

Wimper shuddered and drove his lathering horse with quirt and spur. Where were the rest of his men? Cut off between the herd and fire? Or gone down beneath that sea of slashing hoofs? Wimper dared not think, but feared the worst.

With heartbreaking effort, nose and tail outthrust in one straight forward-hurtling line above its pistoning legs, Wimper's horse held its own against that thundering horde behind.

When next he looked only one man rode behind him and the horns of the leading steers were scant inches from the rump of this white-faced fellow's mount.

Wimper strained the aching muscles that were driving his spurs and quirt. But his horse was giving its utmost now; not another fraction of speed could the gallant animal produce.

The minutes clicked by with drumming beat. Cold sweat broke out on Wimper's back and neck and face as a sobbing cry went up behind and was instantly blotted in the noise of that wild stampede. Smoke, hurled by the rising wind across the backs of the snorting, bellowing herd, swirled about his head and brought tears streaming from his smarting eyes.

Some minutes passed and he dared another glance behind. He could see the lightning playing across that sea of tossing horns. The herd was gaining, gaining, gaining, and—

"Gawd!"

He rode alone!

Chill rain came down in torrents, lashed stinging across his ashen face. He knew that he was in the pass now even though he could not see a thing on either side or even ahead, for the clatter of hoofs rose hard from off its rocky floor. Even the flickering glow of the fire-licked grasses was left behind by the canyon's twistings and only his horse's instinct served as guide through this pouring murk.

The jarring thunder of pounding hoofs rang loud in his ears, hurled forward by the gusty wind that plastered his sodden shirt against his back. His heart was in his throat; he was shaking as with ague.

Then suddenly his horse had lost its stride, was skidding on the slimy gumbo under foot and was going down. . . . His equine scream was tangled with Wimper's sobbing cry. Then both were lost beneath the hoofs of the lumbering steers.

CHAPTER THIRTEEN

T HAT storm is comin' bloody fast," Jones shouted in Shane's ear as, the fire started, they headed for their horses on the run. "Be doin' dam' well if we make that cave where we left the girl before she strikes!"

Shane wasted no time in words but sprinted faster.

They reached the horses. Shane's blue roan was moving at a hard run when he settled his lean frame in the saddle and his other foot found the swinging stirrup. Then he spoke, the wind tearing words from his mouth, "All hell's goin' . . . come apart . . . cattle see that fire!"

A malicious grin curled Bless Jones' lips. " 'Ere's one night I'm bloody well glad I ain't no blarsted rustler!"

They rode in silence then, their upper bodies bent forward over their ponies' necks. This onrushing storm was going to play hell with the mountain trails, and they knew it and had no desire for it to overtake them out of shelter.

"Reckon this'll teach that blarsted Lume ter mind 'is P's an' Q's!"

"I allow it'll mebbe save the bulk of some rancher's cattle," Shane roared back. "Between the fire an' the storm them steers are goin' to cover some rearward territory, or my name ain't Sudden Shane."

He felt no more regret for the possible loss of life their move might spell than he had felt for the deaths of other men his .45 had heralded. The men who were with those cattle were rustlers, thieves who were constantly preying on the small-spread ranchers who strove so valiantly to keep body and soul together in the bleak and desolate wilderness of this mountain country. Should proper authorities have captured Lume's long-loop riders, and an honest and unprejudiced trial gone through, they would have hanged. His move in stampeding the stolen herd had saved not only the ranchers but the state a deal of money. He felt no modicum of regret for what he'd done, but only a coldly grim satisfaction.

They arrived at last within sight of the cave, yet still a good half mile away. Then rain lashed down across their shoulders and stung their faces and though they managed to get on their slickers without halting, their clothes were sopping wet before they could get them on.

They rode in shivering silence, listening to the wild beat of the windflung rain, and the squashy *plopping* of their ponies' hoofs. Shane huddled forward in his saddle, squinted eyes peering through the murky, watery gloom ahead in vain endeavor to catch a glimpse of the campfire they'd built inside the cave for Lize.

It seemed an eternity to Shane before they sloshed to a halt before the hole-pierced cliff that once had been the home of forgotten cave-dwellers. Shane's eyes abruptly widened. He could catch the reflected play of the firelight now where it struck tangently from the entrance, and in its glow he could see that Lize Corbin's horse was gone from where he'd left it hobbled!

He left the saddle with a ripped-out curse, struck the shaley ground on skidding bootheels and vanished inside the cave to reappear a moment later with a face gone ghastly white.

"She's gone!" he blurted crazily. "Gone—*Gone!* Some polecat bastard's been here an' carried her off! Oh, Jones, I'll cut his *heart* out when I get him!" his voice was filled with a merciless hate.

Bless Jones returned his stare in stunned surprise. His expression seemed to say that such a thing was impossible. "Gone?" he echoed. "Then it's Lume or some'v 'is 'ellions 'as got 'er!"

Shane's face, in the reddish glow of the firelight, was twisted by his emotions. Hot rage was gleaming from his smoky eyes that were alive with the portent of imminent volcanic action. There came a drive to his voice that made Jones stiffen in his saddle:

"We're headin' for Tortilla Flat; if we don't find Lize Corbin, or if a hair of her head's been harmed, by Gawd we'll take that camp apart an' hang Jarson Lume from the awning of his own damned joint!"

The shortest way to Tortilla Flat from where they were was by way of the old stage road from Phoenix, which passed through Mesa, Apache Junction, Youngsburg and Mormon Flat. Shane intended to strike the road somewhere between Youngsburg and Mormon Flat. It was almost morning now; they could not possibly reach their destination before the darkness that now was thinning to a watery gray gloom closed again about this desolate land. But, determined to make the best time possible, Shane—followed by the faithful ex-Cockney—started at once.

There was no trail where Shane was leading, not even the veriest ghost of a trail. He picked his way by instinct and traversed canyons apparently choked with rock rubble from ancient slides; he crossed barriers that would have stopped another man before he started. Up and down he led and round and about great bluffs and mesas. The storm passed on or they left it behind and the sun shone down upon their backs with unrelenting fury while they pushed doggedly on with neither food nor water. Only Shane's iron will kept them going when they came to the bleak and shimmering alkaline expanse of some ancient lake bed. Heat waves crinkled and folded above its forgotten floor and the white, clinging alkaline dust rose about them in clouds that brought tears from their reddened, stinging eyes and made breathing, even through the screening folds of their neckerchiefs, an almost unbearable ordeal.

Jones asked once if Shane thought they were lost. Shane growled back some sardonic reply which Jones did not catch. But after that Jones kept still.

Their lips grew parched and cracked as the long hot hours dragged inchingly past. Their nostrils burned as though scorched by the flames of hell itself, and their tongues became immovable cottony lumps whose swelling threatened to stop their breathing entirely. Dust-devils, whipped up by a furnace wind, whirled across their path and one came apart above them, literally showering them with its cargo of super-heated grit. Long since their eyes had closed to merest squinting slits, their eyeballs seared by the burning glare. Talk was impossible and neither man attempted it.

Noon finally came. The torture of the lake bed lay behind. Ahead lay the scarcely lesser torture of the blistering dun expanse of cactus-dotted desert. Above them a buzzard serenely circled the brassy sky on outspread wings while the flaying sun beat down without respite.

They did not stop. They knew their horses could not last much longer, but a glance at Shane's face told Jones that to remonstrate—even if he succeeded in making himself understood—would be useless. Shane's eyes held but a single purpose and it was as unswervable as adamant. He meant to reach Tortilla Flat and Lume in the shortest possible time, and the grim-clenched line of his stubborn jaw forecast that all hell was not going to stop him.

The hot rays of the burning sun beat down upon this arid land like brassy hammers. Shane led doggedly on, grim as some ancient mariner. Their ponies gave out before the desert was spanned and they abandoned them, staggering on afoot.

Late afternoon found them studying the tracks of three horses leading across a lone, pine-shaded plateau. There were puffs of earth before and behind each print, showing the animals had been moving at a smart gallop.

Shane stared at Jones from red-rimmed bloodshot eyes. "That's them," he croaked, and went lurching on. Somehow, somewhere, Jones found the guts to follow, though his face was puffed and black beneath its crust of alkali dust.

Ten minutes later they came to a spring among some rocks. Shane drank cautiously, barely wetting his long-numb lips. He jerked Jones back with guttural noises when the man would have sated his fearful thirst; fought with him, forced him to do as he himself was doing.

An hour passed while they rested and washed the sticky white grime from face and neck and brows. They had no energy to spare in cuffing the grit from their clothing, but lay stretched out in intolerable weariness on the needle-carpeted ground beneath the pines.

When the hour had worn itself out Shane got to his feet. "C'mon," he croaked. "We're movin'," and started off, his hat shoved back from his forehead to let the evening breeze lap coolly across its sweaty surface.

As long shadows from the distant mountains reached down across the country they sighted a tiny ranch tucked away in a hollow. When they got near Shane gruffed a greeting. A man stepped from the cabin door, a rifle held loosely in the crook of his arm. He eyed them scowlingly, not offering to speak.

"We wanta buy coupla hosses," Shane got out with effort.

"Ain't got no broncs fer sale."

Shane's eyes swept across a pole corral inside which half a dozen horses eyed them curiously.

"How 'bout them?"

"Not fer sale," the surly ranchman said without compromise.

Shane did not compromise either. "Yo're a liar!"

Up came the rancher's rifle. His jaw swung forward

menacingly. *"Git!"* There were pale fires in his cat-like yellow gaze.

Shane half turned as though to go. His right hand slapped leather. Livid flame reached out from the explosion at his hip. The rifleman crashed back against the cabin wall with a bullet through his chest. The rifle clattered on the steps.

But the fellow was game. One hand clawed desperately for the belt gun in the tied-down holster on his leg. The flat sharp crack of Shane's pistol made a faint flutter of sound in the immense silence of the gathering dusk. The boss of this hidden ranch sagged back against the wall, slid down it to a sitting posture, then toppled forward to sprawl inertly across the dusty steps.

Shane pushed fresh cartridges in his gun, lips framed in a snarl. "Go hunt us up some saddles, Bless. We'll want two of these broncs apiece."

Fifteen minutes later they rode out at a fast canter, each leading an extra horse. Night's thickening shadows swiftly hemmed them. . . .

In the east a lop-sided yellow moon climbed into the purple sky. The stars paled before its argent glory.

From a shelf of rimrock Shane and Jones stared down upon a winding, pale white ribbon of road that led up out of a dim-seen valley. They had changed horses several times in getting here and they had made good time. They were looking down upon the stage road to Phoenix, about two miles west of Tortilla Flat. Two unknown riders had just swung onto the trail below them. Shane's interest in them seemed strangely acute to Jones.

"Think yer know 'em?" he asked softly.

Shane said in a tiny whisper, "I'm bettin' one of 'em's Stone Latham; just his build an' sits the saddle similar."

"What yer reckon they're up ter?"

"Quien sabe?" Shane said, and shrugged. "However—we'll soon find out. Listen!"

Through the cold crisp moonlit air came the sound of wagon wheels, the jingling of chains and the clupping of pulling horses. The sounds came from the direction of Tortilla Flat. A moment later they saw the stage lurch round a bend and come careening toward them. They could hear above the wagon-squeaks and the plopping pound of hoofs the singing snap of the driver's whip. They could see the shotgun guard upon the box.

"Look," Shane whispered, and following his pointing hand Jones saw that the two men in the road had vanished.

"Stick-up!" he muttered hoarsely.

"Shhh! Looks like a double-cross to me."

The stage came steadily on, the horses pulling against their harness on the steadily-rising grade. Shane and Jones could hear the driver's profane talk; could make snatches of it out above the rattle of the wheels. The coach lurched violently once as a wheel dropped into a chuckhole, careened toward the abyss that bounded the road's outer edge and seemed for an instant in danger of going off. But with lurid oaths and skillful handling of the lines the driver kept his four-horse team moving and the coach still on the road.

Jones took a deep breath. "Whew!"

Shane did not take his eyes from the scene below.

"Close," came the driver's voice, and he spat over the wheel nonchalantly. "But I've had closer," he confided to the guard. "Dang lucky they ain't no passengers aboard. Reckon 'twould have scairt the liver outen 'em. Git-ap, there!"

Two mounted shadows stepped into the road ahead of the lumbering stage. There was a glint of metal and a lance of flame. Another. Two reports rocked against the rimrock where Shane and Jones crouched watching. One of the lead horses was down. The shotgun guard bent double and toppled from the box. An oath left the driver's lips and he hurriedly raised his hands as the stage lurched to a violent stop against the heap of kicking horses.

Three more shots rang out and the horses' struggles ceased.

"Anybody in that stage?" came Latham's voice.

"No." The driver's tone was quavery as though he knew how close he sat to death.

The faces of the hold-up men were masked, but anyone would have recognized Latham's voice, had they ever heard it. "Must be figurin' to quit the country," Shane thought grimly.

"All right," snapped Latham's voice, "come down outa it!"

"Comin'," the driver gulped meekly and, wrapping his lines about the brake, stepped gingerly down over the wheel and stood with his hands stretched as far above his head as Nature would permit.

The man with Latham dismounted and started toward the stage, very likely with the intention of relieving it of some of its more valuable cargo. But it will never be known for sure. Shane had seen enough.

"Drop that bird," he muttered close to Jones' ear. "I'll take care of Latham."

In the moon's soft glow that washed the road with blue radiance, Jones took aim and fired. The sound of the shot tore a hole through the night. Latham's companion in thievery doubled up and crumpled forward in the dust. Latham's horse reared with snorting fright just as Shane fired and took Shane's bullet from end to end. Down it went in a thrashing heap. But even as it fell Stone Latham left its back and, amid a very hail of lead, dashed to his companion's mount, vaulted into the saddle and was gone just as a mass of fleecy cloud passed below the moon and snuffed its light.

"Which way'd 'e go?" snarled Jones, peering wildly over the rimrock's edge. "Wot did yer want ter let 'im git away fer?"

Shane snorted. "I didn't do it a-purpose, an' you can stick a pin in that!"

Just then, with the same suddenness with which it had passed from sight, the moon surged free of its entangling cloud and again illumined the ribbon of road. It showed Stone Latham spurring madly along the trail to camp.

"There 'e goes, the blarsted gopher!" Jones growled. "Let me at my 'oss!"

"Hold on," Shane said, and grabbed him by the shirt. "Take it easy. Latham don't know who blew his game up Bitter Crick. Wait—we'll stand a better chance in town. We'll get him in Tortilla. Let's go down an' habla with that driver."

But when Jones had got cooled down sufficiently to listen, the stage driver was no longer to be seen. Evidently he had had all the shooting he was wanting for one night and had taken his chance and ducked.

"Wot abaht the gold?"

"If there's any on the stage, it prob'ly belongs to Lume. T'hell with it! C'mon, we're headin' for town."

CHAPTER FOURTEEN

GREED, greed, greed! Shane thought disgustedly as he rode through the soft, enfolding moonlight toward a reckoning with Lume. He would be glad to shake forever from his boots the dust of this turbulent Tortilla Flat! Greed, greed, greed! People round this country had gold colic so bad it was all they thought or talked about!

The mood of a moment ago was gone and the driving anger of that time when he had found Lize Corbin no longer in the cave was on him. The reckoning with Lume, he told himself, could not come too soon. Lume had done his best to get him killed off; Lume had stolen for a pittance old Obe Struthers' mine, and had robbed many another of his rightful property. And now Lume had overstepped the safety mark. He had had Lize Corbin kidnapped! The day of retribution was about to dawn!

And Shane, in this dark mood of reprisal, certainly looked like some destroying angel. Seen in the moonlight his face was cold and taut; his gleaming eyes were

150

slightly squinted, the bold curve of his hawk's beak nose was more pronounced than ever, and his lips were a tight lean gash.

He could see Lize Corbin's vision ever before him on the road. Beautiful and fragrant as a rose, it was, the stormy blue of her eyes now a-shine with impassioned tenderness as when he'd held her in his arms after the killing of Tularosa. And always, across her shoulder, mocked the cold, sardonic face of Jarson Lume!

He was like a blight on all this land, Shane thought bitterly. The man's power for evil was a terrible thing. This country had been slumbering with the peace of centuries before Lume's coming; Tortilla Flat had been nothing but a trading post, a watering spot for cowboys and miners passing through the mountains to stop a while and exchange range gossip while the former cooled their saddles and the latter rested their homely jacks and burros.

And now look at it! ran his sombre thoughts. A first class hell-hole, if he'd ever seen one! Honkytonks, gambling establishments, saloons, brothels! Killings were so commonplace they no longer attracted attention—leastways, not from anyone but tenderfeet. And a stage-robber wore the marshal's badge!

"Wot yer figgerin' ter do when we get ter town?" Jones presently asked.

"I'm goin' to hunt up Jarson Lume, find out what they've done with Lize, then give Lume what he's been askin' for ever since he got here!"

"Kinder tall order, wot? 'Adn't yer better take 'em one at a time?"

"You keep out of this, Jones," Shane scowled grimly. "This is my fight, an' I don't want no help nor need any. I'll show those damned scorpions a thing or two they'll be a right smart while forgettin'!"

Jones looked at him sideways and began to hum, "Oh, the king of France, he put on his pants—"

Shane's grim lips relaxed in a sudden smile. "Well, mebbe I did sound kinda boastful," he admitted, "but I'm allowin' I'm big enough to handle this situation without no help. An' there ain't no sense nohow in you gettin' mixed up in this fracas. You was hired to build a coupla buildin's on that spread I bought an' to help repair some more an' the corrals an' such-like. You wasn't hired for your gun, Bless."

"Well, wot the bloody 'ell do yer think I'm a-carryin' this 'ere smoke-pole fer?" Jones asked indignantly. "Ter scare mosquitoes off? Not 'arf! A fine bloke I'd be ter stand around meek as Moses w'ile them curly wolves got yer ready for the undertaker, wot? Look 'ere, yer glory-'oggin' idjit!— W'en the bullets starts ter flyin', the Earl o' Cockney's li'l son 'Orace aims ter be right w'ere 'e can 'ear their blinkin' w'istles! An' yer can kiss the Stone on that!"

Though it was almost midnight when they reached the town it was plain to Shane and Jones that no citizen was in his bed unless he were held there by a malady or gun-shot wound. The camp's night life was at full blast and a noisy blare of raucous sound destroyed the quiet serenity of the nocturne breeze.

Overhead, far up in the purple heavens, the stars

peered down with awe. The dusty road ahead of Shane was splashed with crisscross bars of yellow light that poured from open doors and windows, for though the night was cool the activities of the larger part of Tortilla Flat's inhabitants were badly in need of the soothing influence of pure, clean air.

Dismounting at the hitch rack fronting the Square Deal, Shane and Jones flipped their reins about the rail and strode within. Shane's firm, unhurried stride carried him to where a blank wall was at his back, and Jones took up a position there beside him. Both men manufactured cigarettes while accustoming their eyes to the glare of fifty lamps.

The atmosphere was heavy with the odors of leather, stale liquor, sweat, smoke and dust. The cigarette smoke swirled in heavy stratas a foot beneath the balcony ceiling, and the air above that level was blue with it. There were oaths and raucous laughter, flashing smiles and gleaming, hateful eyes; and occasionally the angry cry of some dance hall girl rose indignantly through the babelous din, while over all resounded the banged-out notes of an old off-key piano.

Here and there along the line of men bellying the ornate bar, space was left for a drunken companion who no longer had the use of his legs but sat sprawled limply upon the footrail of gleaming brass.

Above the gaming tables were hunched great dark-faced cowmen; big, bronzed, serious men whose cheeks were networks of intent wrinkles and whose gnarled hands were never far from the butts of ready weapons. The stakes were high. One false move on an opponent's part would have brought his death in an avenging blast of gunfire.

Shane and Jones leaned their backs against a wall and watched the room through squinted eyes while they languidly puffed their smokes.

A big breed went slouching past, his swarthy face writhed in a scowl, one arm in a dirty sling. The minute remainder of a cornhusk cigarro showed between his thick lips and a burning resentment was in his glance.

Olive-skinned women, slender creatures of sensuous rhythm glided by, their red lips parted in flashing smiles, their luring eyes twin pools of slumberous dusk neath sweeping lashes.

Through the wavering smoke Shane saw a pair of men leave Lume's private room beneath the balcony stairs. They did not observe him and Jones smoking placidly against the wall across the room, but headed toward them, making for the swinging doors.

Jones said from a corner of his mouth, "Hin a bloody 'urry, if yer arskin' me!"

The first man was a solidly-built gent, muscular and heavy of face. Bad thought through turbulent years had drawn down a corner of his mouth and creased it in a perpetual sneer and there was a sneaking droop to his big shoulders. As he came hurrying forward his hands swung close to the .45s he wore on either hip. It was Birch Alder Shane was staring at, though he had no means of knowing this; nor, had he known, would it have made any difference.

For Shane's glance went swiftly past Alder and came to rest in narrowing intensity on the man behind. He was tall, rawboned and gaunt. He had a lantern jaw and heavy eyes beneath the rakish tilt of a down-pulled hat-brim. He moved with a saddlebound swagger that just now seemed filled with wrath. His dark and lean-carved face showed anger, too. His lips were set in a vicious snarl.

Shane shoved abruptly free of the wall against which he had been leaning, hands hanging loosely at his sides. Alder did not notice. But the other did. Shane saw the bold eyes swinging toward him, focus upon his face and harden, narrow. The snarl slid off the fellow's lips as he swung to a sudden halt, and his right hand brushed the polished walnut of his gun-butt.

Then, leisurely, the man came on, lips curving in a cynical grin. He came urbanely on until he stood facing Shane with right thumb hooked in gunbelt across a three-foot interval.

"Howdy, catawampus. Thirsty weather, ain't it?"

"I know a place that's thirstier," Shane drawled coldly. "Latham, where's Lize Corbin at?" His glance beat hard as flint against Stone Latham's high-boned cheeks.

Latham met his scrutiny amusedly, antagonistic mockery in his gleaming eyes.

"Why ask me?" he sneered. " 'F I was to foller all the peregrinations of a hustlin' skirt like Li—"

His voice broke off in a startled grunt as Shane's right fist rocked hard against his jaw. All the pent-up hate and bitter fury was in that blow, and it smashed Stone Latham backward to his knees. Before he could recover, Shane's left came up beneath his chin and

155

sprawled him moveless on his back with glazing eyes.

A stunned sort of stillness gripped the hall for a space of seconds. Then, Alder, who had caught the last of the scene from the tail of his eyes, let a hand streak hipward for his gun. Other hands sped holsterward for vengeance.

"Kill the damned outlander!"

"Rub 'im out!"

"Get him, boys!" snarled Alder, and jerked his weapon free.

Shane's hand slapped leather as gun thunder shook the room, awaking monstrous echoes that jarred the swirling smoke and drove bystanders headlong in search of nearest shelter.

Black holes appeared like magic in the wall above and about Shane's crouching back. With slitted eyes he crouched there in the garish light of fifty lamps. The swift tattoo of his belching gun drove men frantically for doors and windows. Birch Alder, clutching at his stomach in sobbing agony, had hardly struck the floor before the place was cleared; deserted, save for himself and the grinning Jones and the three still forms that sprawled grotesquely near.

Bless Jones abruptly swore. "'E's gorn!" he snarled excitedly.

"What—"

"*Latham!* 'E's flitted like a bloody bird!"

True enough; Latham, indeed, was gone—vanished in those few tumultuous seconds!

"The back room!" Shane snapped, and headed for it stuffing fresh cartridges in the emptied chambers of his pistol, bootheels thumping hollowly.

Jones beat him to it, flung back the door and cursed. "Empty! The bloody sparrow's 'opped!"

"Quick!" Shane cried, sprinting for the swinging doors. "Don't let 'em get away!"

But they were too late. Dimming with receding distance they could hear the muffled pound of fleeing hoofs as they stood by the hitch rack fronting Lume's Square Deal.

The crowd came surging back. Shane grabbed a man and hissed:

"Where's Jarson Lume? Talk quick, fella, 'cause I'm in a sod-pawin' mood an' I'd as lief horn you as not!"

With chattering teeth the fellow shook his head. "Good cripes," he gasped, "don't take it out on me! *I* ain't seen Lume for fifteen minutes!"

"Where is he?" Shane glared wildly at the crowd who shrank back before the things to be read in his blazing eyes. "*Where is he?* Speak up quick, by Gawd, or I'll tear this camp apart!"

"What's wrong, pardner?" growled a bearded, booted fellow in a red flannel shirt. "You look some riled up. Someone stole yore lollypop?"

"Some of Lume's stinkin' hellions've kidnapped Lize Corbin!"

Low growls of anger rose. But a man near Shane sneered knowingly. "I reckon," he said, "she won't be mindin' such a heap. Lize, she's used to sleepin' ou—"

Shane's right fist spun the man headlong in the dusty road. Shane's cold voice lashed the crowd like icy water:

"If there's any more white-livered sneaks in this stinkin' camp aimin' to insult a decent woman behind her back, now's the time to do it!"

A frozen silence held the group. One or two shifted their feet uneasily. Several surreptitiously departed.

Shane's cold drawl was contemptuous. "Then get the hell out of here."

"Wot next?" Jones asked with a tickled grin.

"Look over these nags that's tied up here an' pick us out a couple good ones that's long on endurance an' look like they might have a fairish amount of speed. I'm allowin' I've got a hankerin' to cast my eyes round Lume's establishment once more afore we roll our tails. Be with you in three shakes. Get some canteens an' see that they're filled with water. Rustle a coupla saddle-bags of food, too, while you're at it. The trail we're takin' mightn't have no stops."

Wheeling then, Shane went back inside the deserted Square Deal. A bartender stood staring idiotically at the dead men on the floor. A sawbones was bending anxiously above Birch Alder's prostrate form. Shane paid them no attention, but took the balcony stairs three at a time. One by one he went through the rooms that faced its railing. Three were empty. Four held terrified, huddling girls who shrank away from his burning glance. Then he came to number ten—the room he was to have shared with the late Bill Halleck.

It, too, was empty. Shane was about to turn away when his eyes caught sight of a crumpled bit of paper slightly protruding from beneath the pillow on the bunk.

Bending, he picked it up and smoothed it out upon a knee. Three scrawled words leapt to his glance like tongues of flame:

Lume— help— Lize—

He thrust the paper mechanically in his pocket. The muscles of his jaws stood out in tense rigidity. So Lume *had* got her, had he? Shane's lips tightened grimly; cold glints of fury entered his smoky eyes as he swung to the door and out upon the balcony and down the stairs. His boots thumped hollowly in the unaccustomed silence and the tinkling of his big-roweled spurs was like the sound of clashing sabers as he crossed the deserted floor.

The doctor looked up from Birch Alder's motionless body. "I guess he's finished," he said conversationally.

"There'll be a lot more polecats finished before I get through," Shane growled, and pushed through the swinging doors into a burst of exploding light. How he escaped that murderous salvo Shane never knew. But something—buck fever, possibly—might have unsettled Mell's aim. For Mell it was; Shane saw him crouching at the porch-edge with a shotgun in his hands.

Mell had no chance to use the gun again. Like magic Shane's gun seemed to leap to his hand and bark. Mell went over backwards off the porch with a bullet between his eyes.

From across the street Jones came running awkwardly, a pair of saddlebags flapping from each shoulder; skin water bags filled his hands. "Wot's up? Wot's up 'ere, eh? Wot's orl this shootin' abaht?" he panted.

Shane took a pair of saddlebags and one of the canteens. "Where's the broncs?"

"Right 'ere," Jones said, and led the way to where a pair of wall-eyed, long-legged bronchos stamped restlessly beside the rail.

" 'Ll them suit?"

"Yeah. Let's get goin'," said Shane, stepping into the saddle atop a blue roan. "Lume an' whoever's with him prob'ly took the same direction as Latham."

"That's right, fella," a scrawny youth said, nodding. "I seen 'em. Haff a hour ago, it was. They was headin' off to'ards Globe. There's a short cut—"

But Shane was waiting for no more. The blue roan lunged forward beneath his prodding spurs. With a wink at the gaping boy, Jones too put spurs to his mount and went pelting in Shane's wake.

CHAPTER FIFTEEN

THE lofty spires of the Superstition Range were etched ruggedly black against the starry skyline. For what seemed like centuries Shane and Bless Jones rode in silence, the vast quiet of the open spaces hemming them like a shroud, and the only sounds to lend accompaniment to the clatter of hoofs were the creak of saddle leather and the occasional jingling of spur chains.

Slowly the moon grew dimmer. One by one the stars

faded and vanished from the brightening heavens. In the cold, pale light of dawn they stepped stiffly from their saddles. Jones walked the horses up and down to prevent their cooling too swiftly while Shane cast round for sign.

A bleak wind rattled eerily through the chaparral as Shane examined the trail. Tired and weary as he was, the smoky eyes beneath his puckered brows were keenly alert. He well knew the possibilities they ran of being ambushed. A thing like that would find appeal in Latham's Indian blood.

Striding out upon a bare escarpment overlooking a tiny valley far below, Shane pondered the fact that only one set of fresh tracks showed in this trail. Where had Lume gone with the girl? Did Latham know and was he short-cutting in an effort to head them off? But why should he? What, Shane wondered, was the connection between Latham and Lume? Surely there was something more to it than the mere relationship of outlaw chieftain and right-bower henchman; no mere lieutenant, no matter how privileged, would dare such familiarity and insolence toward Lume as Latham had more than once exhibited, Shane felt. Therefore, he reasoned, there must be some deeper, stronger tie between these men. But what?

Still eying the valley through a rift in the morning mist, Shane shrugged. The roaring surge of anger that had taken him so recklessly into Lume's camp and dive a few short hours ago with the desire to rend and maim had cooled. The desire still pulsed through his veins, but it was a yearn now purged of impulse—a controlled

161

anger, a deep abiding hate that would brook no obstacle to its deadly path.

He rejoined Jones where he walked their horses up and down a narrow stretch of trail.

"Find anythin'?"

"Latham's ridin' a cold trail. Either he's not figurin' to join up with Lume's party, or else he's takin' some kinda short cut to where he thinks they're headin' for. Anyhow, we're stickin' to Latham; I've a hunch he knows what he's doin'. Let's go."

The sun climbed into a cloudless sky, its rays burning brighter with each passing moment, warming the air rarified and chilled by mountain night. Half an hour passed and only the occasional click of a horse's shoe against a rock or pebble betrayed their presence on the needle-carpeted trail along the timbered ridges. They climbed steadily higher into the mountains. The horses' hearts thumped softly against their knees.

Shane's blue roan set the pace, a swift running walk that often broke into a trot where the going was easier—a pace that would put long miles behind a rider between sun-up and dark, yet leave his mount with plenty of steam.

It was nearing noon when Shane, riding in the lead, suddenly drew in his horse and pointed silently. A group of tracks sheared into their trail from the north-west. Three separate sets of tracks, Shane pointed out. Jones nodded.

Shane said, "Latham guessed right. I'm allowin' he's saved us a heap of time, Bless. I'm allowin' them prints belongs to Lume an' his party. One would be Lume's

162

horse, another Lize's. That means he's only got one man with him. He sure must have left town hellity-larrup to be travelin' so light. Somethin' must have give him a scare."

Jones nodded. "Yer reckon it was Latham?"

"Can't say. It's a cinch Latham wasn't in town when Lume pulled out with the girl."

"Mebbe they've split," Jones suggested hopefully. "I ain't never put no great store in this talk abaht honor amongst thieves."

"Well, Latham's on their trail, anyhow. An' that's the main thing. We better be shovin' on."

"Where d'yer reckon they're goin'?" Jones asked after fifteen minutes of silent riding. "That feller back in Tortilla said Globe, didn't 'e?"

"He wouldn't know nothin' about Lume's plans. He said they'd hit out on the Globe trail. But these tracks now are pointin' dead on for Silver King. I'm thinkin' we'll be findin' 'em there."

"Well, 'ere's 'opin'!" Jones said "My backbone's a rubbin' up ag'in' m' blinkin' stomach an' if we 'ave ter ride much further I'm goin' ter fall plumb asleep right 'ere in m' bloody saddles."

Half an hour later as they were rounding a bend of a rock-choked canyon, a scant two miles from Silver King, the sultry afternoon quiet was shattered by a shot. Something tugged at Shane's neckerchief—it was that close—as the report beat back against the towering walls in dimming echoes.

The abruptness of Jones' stopping sent up tiny bursts of dust. "Look out!" he yelled.

But already Shane had marked the tiny puff of smoke ballooning above the glistening barrel of a rifle in a clump of rocks three hundred yards ahead.

The pony lunged beneath him with hip-jolting violence to his sudden drive of spurs. Jones' voice died out in the pound of the big roan's hoofs as Shane hurled his bronc toward the ambusher's covert with whitened cheeks, teeth bared in a savage grin.

His racing palm smacked gun-butt as the dry-gulcher broke from cover. The hammer rolled beneath his thumb. The loud reports churned up like thunder between the canyon walls. The ambusher had dropped to a knee and was sighting down his rifle. Pale flame stabbed from its muzzle. Lead splashing off his saddle horn jerked a grunt from Shane. Abruptly the blue roan came apart beneath him. Shane hurled himself from the saddle as the bronc went down in a crashing fall.

Shane lit rolling, gun still clenched in hand. He was up on his feet in an instant, hardly a hundred yards separating himself from the dry-gulcher who now was firing with desperate haste, fearful of being caught in his own trap.

Lead ripped through Shane's vest, tugged at his hat, jarred his balance as a heel ripped loose from his left boot. Then he was sprinting forward awkwardly in the wake of the fleeing killer who was making for a horse that stood at a little distance on spraddled legs, its sides a smear of blood from the slash of cruel spurs.

As the man threw himself into the saddle Shane fired again, carefully, deliberate—grim malice in his heart.

The man's rising leg missed going over the saddle by

inches. Shane could see the shudder that shook his slender frame. Then he was crumpling groundward, one foot still hooked in the stirrup. The horse was too spent to buck. It stood listless with down-hung head as though anchored by its motionless master. It did not even turn its eyes as Shane, followed by Jones, approached.

Shane released the fellow's foot from the stirrup. Jones came up cursing soulfully, the while he lamented his luck in not having had a hand in the fracas.

"Mex, eh?"

Shane nodded wearily. Reaction was on him now as it always was after a killing. He felt a little sick at his stomach and strove to hide the fact behind a scowl. "Know him?"

Jones bent down for a closer look. Nothing squeamish about *his* stomach. "I've seen 'im. Name's Pedro Abrilla—one of Jarson's gun-packers. Mean customer with a knife. I seen 'im carve a gent plumb scandalous the night before they run me out of their blarsted camp."

"Lume an' Lize . . ." Shane muttered thoughtfully. "This must be the fella that was ridin' the third horse. An' if this here's the bronc, they sure must have been spreadin' scenery right blurry-like. Looks plumb tuckered out."

"How you figgerin' ter git places now that bloke did in yer 'oss?"

"We're pretty close to Silver King," Shane said, squinting down the canyon. "Guess we better ride double a spell. I'll pick up a horse soon's we get there.

165

An' I reckon we better be gettin'—pronto. The trail is warmin' up."

In the Red Hoss Saloon at Silver King Jarson Lume was talking with its proprietor in a back room. Lize was with them, watching them sullenly while they talked.

"Aimin' to put her in the business, Jars?" Red Fogle asked, his lewd glance passing over the girl's figure. "She's a likely baggage an' oughta attract plenty trade."

Jarson Lume's voice, though well-modulated, was icy. "No. This lady is my wife, Red."

"S'cuse *me!*" Fogle was rising hastily and clawing at his cast-iron hat when Lize Corbin's voice lashed vibrantly:

"Yo' a damn liar, Jarson Lume!"

Fogle stared uncertainly from the girl's flushed cheeks to the sardonic smile on Lume's thin, bloodless lips. "Well," he said dubiously, "anything you folks say is all right with me. I ain't knowin' nothin' about it one way or the other. An', beggin' yore pardon, ma'am, I ain't givin' a damn one way or the other."

Lume chuckled silently. "You always was handy with the right answer, Red. Fix us up some grub. We're half-starved. After that find us a place upstairs where we can sleep. We've had a damn long ride. I left Pete Abrilla on the backtrail a ways. Keep your eyes peeled for him. 'F anybody else comes round askin' for me, keep yore lip buttoned tight. An' let me know."

Fogle winked. "I get yuh, boss. How's tricks up Tortilla way?"

"I'm through with that camp," Lume said shortly, and

changed the subject. "Any of the boys in town?"

"Three or four, I reckon. Rest went out on a little shindig las' night an' ain't got back yet. You wantin' to see 'em?"

"Not now—later, mebbe. Rattle your hocks now an' fetch that grub before I fall apart."

With a final admiring glance at Lize, Fogle went out and closed the door.

The minute he was out of sight Lize flared: "If y'u think y'u are goin' to get me into one of them upstairs rooms with y'u yo' plumb crazy as hell!"

Lume grinned wolfishly. "Shucks, you'll be lookin' forward to a little privacy like that inside a month," he sneered. "You better make up your mind to marry me an' do it quick if you're so damned virtuous. 'Cause, one way or another, I'm aimin' to have you. An' when Jarson Lume makes up his mind to have a thing, he has it! Think it over, Lize."

Scorn and loathing were intermingled in Lize Corbin's stormy glance. "Y'u'll never get *me*—I'd kill myself first!"

"You ain't goin' to get no chance," Lume chuckled. "I ain't lettin' you out of my sight till the knot's been tied."

"Y'u—y'u *beast!*"

"Better save them endearin' terms till after we get hitched up," he smirked.

After they had eaten and Lume had seen Lize locked securely in an upstairs room from which he had assured himself there could be no escape, he came downstairs again and drew Red Fogle to one side, where it would be impossible for other customers to overhear.

"Red," he studied Fogle's face intently, "d'you know a man called 'Whisk' Lipari?"

"Short, stocky, black-faced hombre?"

Lume nodded.

"I know him well enough," Fogle admitted cautiously. "What about him?"

"Know if he's in town?"

Fogle considered. "I reckon he is," he finally said, pursing his heavy lips.

"Where can I find him?"

Fogle's eyebrows arched a trifle, then drew down in a beetling scowl. "What kind of a deal you got in mind?"

"There are times," Lume pointed out significantly, "when ignorance is sure the height of bliss, Red. This here is one of those times."

Lights glinted dully in the resort-keeper's glance. He drummed upon the bar with nervous fingers, took a deep breath and let it slowly out.

"Well," he said, as though washing his hands of the business, "I reckon you know what yo' doin', Jars. If you was to wander over to the Gold Gun yo' curiosity might get satisfied." With the words he turned his broad back and strolled huffily away.

Jarson Lume grinned sardonically, pulled his hat rakishly down across one eye and left the place.

Outside the afternoon sun sent its brassy rays down slanchways across the town, sending the elongated, distorted shadows of its flimsy buildings flat and black across the dust-choked road. Heat waves lay in stifling stratas above the blistering boards of its plank walks, above the sand-scoured and sun-grayed wooden awnings. Long shadows bathed the distant mountain-sides in a mantle of sombre purple.

Jarson Lume stood before the Red Hoss and let his veiled glance rove the deserted street. It came to a final rest on an establishment obliquely across the way. His lips curled as he looked down at the bottle-like sheen with which he had, but a few short minutes ago, managed to imbue his boots. With a shrug, then, he strode out across the squalid dust.

When he stepped inside the Gold Gun's swinging doors he swiftly got his back against a dirty wall and, from between slitted lids, sent a searching glance stabbing through the smoky half-light.

There had been laughter in the place but it had quieted at his entrance. Jarson Lume was tempted to press the white 'kerchief, peeping from the breast pocket of his black frock coat, to his nose as he let his glance play over the motley group of sweating humanity that was ranged along the bar. But he repressed the impulse.

A man in a pinto vest and frazzled corduroy trousers tucked into cowhide boots detached himself from his unsavory companions and, with a significant jerk of expressive eyes, moved toward a rear door. Lume followed.

He found himself in a bare back room whose only furnishings were a rough table, two chairs, and great quantities of dust. The man in the pinto vest flashed Lume an intent, appraising glance, then his yellow eyes slid away. He jerked a nod of greeting. "Long time no see."

"How you doin', Lipari? Wallowin' in dinero?"

Lipari grinned—a twisted grimace which did nothing to enhance his ugly looks. "What's on yore mind?"

"I got a chore for you. There's two grand in it."

The yellow eyes did not even blink, but regarded Lume craftily. "Who you got it in for, now?"

"I'm askin' the questions," Lume said, curtly. "Do you figure you can use the dinero—?"

"Did you ever know me when I couldn't?" Lipari countered with a grin.

"Not the point. D'you want it, or shall I pack it some-place else?"

"I'd have to know what mark you was figgerin' to remove. I ain't the man to buy any gent's pig in a poke."

Lume nodded. "I'll spread my cards on the table. Me an' the wife is taken' a little pasear across the country. Someone's on my backtrail. I want 'em stopped—right here. An' permanent."

"Who?"

"You're gettin' damn' partic'lar in your ol' age," Lume snapped coldly.

"I'm findin' that it pays to," was Lipari's blunt come-back. "Who's trailin' you an' the skirt? Come clean, Jars, or I'm passin' up the pot."

"Well, it's no one you know. Fella called Sudden Shane, an' some two-bit gunslick he's picked up."

"Shows you don't know ever'thing, Jars. I reckon you're talkin' about a gent called S. G. Shane. Right?"

Lume was surprised at the other's knowledge, but he kept the fact to himself. With expressionless counte-nance he grunted, "I've heard he gives that name."

"Well, this little chore will cost you real money, Mister. That guy's hell on wheels, an' I've got no hankerin' to be committin' suicide. This chore, Jars, will cost you a cool five grand or the deal's off."

"It's off, then, far as I'm concerned," Lume said, and started for the door.

CHAPTER SIXTEEN

B UT he did not leave immediately. He halted with his hand on the knob and looked back across his shoulder. Whisk Lipari had not changed his position by an inch. He sat sprawled loosely across one of the chairs, thumbs hooked in his suspenders, a wolfish grin on his twisted lips.

"Oh—yeah?" he said, and laughed. It curdled the silence wickedly and snapped a dark flush into Jarson Lume's white cheeks.

Lume's husky tones grew ugly. "Have a care, Lipari. You ain't so *damned* valu'ble to me, you know. There's been other guys that *thought* they were."

"Meanin' where are they now, eh?" Lipari sneered. "I reckon I'll get along—with or without your help."

"I wasn't talkin' about help, my friend."

"Oh." Lights shifted in Lipari's yellow orbs. He drew the left down in an exaggerated wink. "Well, I can get along with or without your damned enmity, too! I ain't been no hired gun all my life, Mister. I've been a lot of things you'll never be; not even if you corner all the gold an' copper mines in this country! Go laff that off."

Lume's scowl ironed out. "All right. Five grand it is,

then. I'll pay you when the job is done."

"Like hell!" sneered Lipari. "You'll pay me now, or get yourself some other sucker. This Shane pilgrim ain't what I'd call a tame gorilla. The guy that downs him is gonna earn what he gets. An' if I'm the guy, I'll do my collectin' in advance. You wouldn't be the first sidewinder that tried to pull a sandy."

Lume's bloodless face grew pinched and venomous. "Are you tryin' to—"

"Stow it," Lipari growled. "Pay up or shut up!"

Hate glowed in Lume's cold eyes. "Lipari," he wrenched out explosively, "you're a dirty damned blood-suckin' leech!"

Lipari's chuckle shrank to a satanic grin. "Blow off all the steam you've a mind to," his drawling voice was contemptuous. "But if you ain't figgerin' to pay, you might as well pull your picket pin now an' drift. Five grand's my price; no more nor less. You gonna pay or ain't you?"

Lume's face was bloated poisonously; his cheeks trembled, so vicious was his wrath. His hand half reached inside his coat so that, for a moment, it seemed he meditated violence. With a sullen oath he drew back the hand, thrusting it instead inside the side pocket of his coat and brought it immediately forth with a thick roll of bills.

"You know," said Lipari sardonically, "a fast draw will beat four aces all of a twitter." And, "You've been packin' that hideout gun so long you're beginnin' to stand slanchways.

"You must be doin' real well, Jars," he added a

moment later, eying the currency. "That roll's big as a wagon hub. You act damn tight for a fella that's fair wallowin' in velvet."

Lume paid no attention but went on counting out the bills. When the pile on the table before Lipari represented five thousand dollars he put the rest—which had not been noticeably diminished—back in his pocket. "See that you do this job right, or I'll be back for an accountin'," he gruffed, and once more started for the door.

As he reached it Lipari's voice came mockingly:

"When you get outside, tell Nogales to come in—I got a job for him."

The door slammed behind Lume viciously.

When Jarson Lume stepped into the street, the sun had dropped from sight behind the towering peaks and long shadows dyed the mountains' flanks with dusk while the summits stood out like crags of liquid gold. But Lume had no eyes for beauty in that form. He crossed the dusty road with determined strides, his face thrust grimly forward, and entered the lamplit interior of the Red Hoss Saloon.

Red Fogle followed him to the rear room where they had sat less than two hours before with Lize.

Lume came at once to the point. "Fogle, you got a man in your string, or a couple of men, who are handy with their smoke-poles and would be glad to earn a bit of cash?"

Fogle's beetling brows went up. "I thought you was figurin' on dealin' with Lipari?"

"You ain't bein' paid to think," Lume said icily. "Have you got the men or not?"

"Yeah, I got a coupla boys that ain't no slouches when it comes to throwin' lead," he admitted, interestedly. "What's up?"

"There's a couple of would-be gunslicks trailin' me," Lume confided, "that I want rubbed out as soon's they show. I aim to be gone before then, but whether I am or not has nothing to do with this deal. Now listen," he added, and proceeded to describe Shane and his companion. How he knew that Jones was with Shane remains a mystery, but he had many ways of finding out the things he took an interest in.

"This job," he concluded gruffly, "pays well—a thousan' bucks apiece. I'm leavin' the cash with you." He counted it out and put it in the other's hand. "Now clear out; I want to do some thinkin'."

But when Fogle had closed the door behind him, Lume's words were certainly belied by his subsequent actions. He removed the gun from the shoulder holster beneath his coat, took the cartridges from its cylinder and replaced them with others taken from his pocket. Then he spun the cylinder critically. Placing the snub-nosed .38 inside his coat pocket he blew out the lamp and left by the rear door, moving with cat-like, noiseless steps.

His way took him down a string of gloomy alleys whose tin-can-littered ground gave off no sign of human presence as he advanced, angling always closer to the street. He at last emerged upon it, but only after carefully scrutinizing the surrounding shadows to be sure that he was not the object of some loiterer's attention.

Like a shadow he flitted across the dusty road, gained the far side without encounter and slunk softly into the gloom-choked space between two buildings. One of these was the Gold Gun. He rounded it, pausing a moment at its rear to make certain he was not observed. Slowly, then, every sinuous nerve strung taut, he advanced on the single window.

At first he thought the room must be deserted, but suddenly realized as he neared it that the window was draped with a heavy blanket. It had not been half an hour before when in that room he had propositioned Whisk Lipari. If Lipari was in there now. . . .

With his right hand tensely gripping the snub-nosed .38 inside his pocket, Lume's left hand found the door unlocked and thrust it open. He could see, almost instantly, the broad squat form of Lipari seated at the table. The money Lume had given him was still piled there before him and it came to Lume that Lipari had been gloating over it.

A flush of rage flamed Lume's cold cheeks; devil's temper lit his eyes.

"Lipari," he whispered hoarsely. And as Lipari whirled, flame bit from the pocket of Lume's black coat. A malicious laugh escaped him as Lipari, eyes bulging, hands clutching at his chest, sagged forward across the table's top. With one swift motion Lume scooped the currency from the table and, stepping back across the threshold, softly closed the door.

Twenty minutes later Jarson Lume stepped once again

inside the swinging doors of Fogle's Red Hoss Saloon. He stepped inside and stopped abruptly, gaze widening then narrowing to regard the half crouched man across the room with gleaming eyes that were hard as flint.

"Well," he purred smoothly into the vibrant silence, "I hadn't expected you so soon—" and was checked by the other's malignant sneer.

"No, you bet you wasn't, you double-crossin', back-bitin', woman-stealin' whelp!" Stone Latham's voice, like the man himself, was coiled like trigger steel. *Where's my wife?*

"Your *wife?*" there was genuine amaze in Lume's startled tones. "What the hell are you talkin' about?"

"Lize Corbin, damn yore soul to hell! *Where is she?* Speak, you white-faced bastard, before I lead yore guts!"

"She asked me to take her out of the country," Lume said calmly, only the tiny fires in his lambent eyes betraying the lashing anger that tore at him, an anger born of hatred of the man before him and jealousy that that man should have had his way with Lize where he himself had failed.

"She didn't say why she wanted to leave," he went on, "except that she found the people hateful, slanderous an' vile—I guess she was thinkin' of *you* when she said the last. But she sure didn't say she'd ever hitched up with you. From the way she talked, I'd judge marryin' you would be the last thing she'd ever think of." There was a cold, calculating mockery in the grin he turned on Latham.

Latham scowled red-eyed and a spot of white

appeared in either cheek. His tall, gaunt form slowly straightened. There was a bold truculence in his glance, and his lips held a cynical curve.

"You're a slick hombre, Jars, taken by an' large. Slick as a sidewinder's belly," he said. "But you're not foolin' me one damn minute longer. *Where's my wife?* I'm not figurin' to ask again."

"She may be your wife," Lume's husky voice with its taunting timbre worked on Latham as a red rag appears to work upon a bull. "She may be your wife." he repeated slowly, nastily, "but she's my woman now— an' I ain't tired of her, yet!"

With a strangled sob Stone Latham, the ever-cautious, clawed wildly for his gun.

From the burned right-hand pocket of Lume's black coat, a streak of flame lanced lividly. Stone Latham's limbs abruptly suspended all lethal motion and a great amazement, not unmixed with fear, distorted his paling face. He took one forward step and staggered. Then the hinges of his knees let go and dropped him in a grotesque heap.

Jarson Lume's cold glance flashed round from face to face. Men quailed back before the message in his blazing eyes. Lume's lips twisted in a contemptuous sneer. "Well, any of you pelicans aimin' to take up where he left off?"

The silence in the Red Hoss bar remained unbroken.

CHAPTER SEVENTEEN

W OULDN'T it p'r'aps be better," Jones asked hesitantly, "if we waited till after dark to go into this bloody Silver King? 'Oo knows wot we might be bargin' inter if we goes rompsin' in there now? Blimey, it fair throws me ter the goose-pimples jest ter be thinkin' of it."

Shane regarded him suspiciously; abruptly chuckled. "Yeah, I'm allowin' you look scared as hell," he said. "But I reckon you are right, at that. We'd be askin' for it if we was to go sashayin' into Silver in broad daylight. Reckon I'm gettin' plumb careless." He squinted out across the yellow earth. "Reckon we better wait till night; wee hours are figgered best for takin' a enemy unawares."

He stepped down from the blown horse's saddle. Jones, too, swung down.

Jones said, "Any'ow, yer wouldn't 'a' got far on that bonerack till 'e 'ad a spot o' rest. That Mex musta pushed 'im cruel 'ard."

Shane nodded. "I reckon." He looked at the dead man's horse with a critical eye. It had shown neither curiosity nor interest at Shane's dismounting. It showed none now, but stood there on spraddled legs, head down, breathing heavily. Sweat trickled from its belly.

Jones squinted to where the sun was sinking from the darkening sky. Its descent was washing the towering canyon walls with gold and in their crevices creating cobalt shadows. "I got a yearnin' void wots pinin' ter be filled," he said, drawing up the slack in his belt. "Any of that grub left?"

"Nope—nary a crumb," Shane answered, grim of voice. He seemed to have relapsed into his customary urbanity again. His face expressed once more the placid patience of one to whom time holds no import. And yet there was that air, that arresting air of confident efficiency about him, an atmosphere of unhurried capability. There was a cool serenity about his smoky eyes that told of a man at peace with his conscience. If he was worried longer about the fate of Lize Corbin, one would never have guessed it from his features.

Jones watched him roll a cigarette with one deft twirl of his fingers—no hesitancy there, no tremble. Jones marveled at his composure, but said nothing, content to leave his thoughts unaired.

Shane unsaddled the Mexican's horse and put him on a rope. Stretching his own long frame Jones proceeded to do likewise. Then, like Shane, he sat down on his bootheels and devoted his time to gravely smoking while the thickening shadows of dusk gathered softly in the canyon.

It was nearing two on the following morning when they approached Silver King, and was so dark—there being no moon—that Shane and his mount were but a shadowy blur three lengths ahead. Jones' lips quirked humorously. A few minutes now and they would know what they would know, he told himself.

The labored breathing of the horses reached out before their nostrils, disturbing the misty murk. Jones had been startled more than once by the eery shadows of tall sahuaros and yellow-stalked sotol shoving up at them out of the gloom, and upon one occasion had even been chagrined to find his gun in hand. He had put it covertly away while watching Shane's broad back with a guise of shame that he had been so callow. In his actions, that is to say. For, personally, he was far from callow, though about his character there did lurk a certain naive charm of which he was totally unconscious. He would very likely have shot any man so reckless as to tell him.

Jones marveled much at Shane's display of horsemanship. He had observed how the slightest flexure of Shane's fingers on the reins held the instant power to stop the dead Mexican's caballo. He recalled how half an hour ago when riding through the desolate waste of sand a coyote's howl had almost spooked his own mount, and how a mere touch of Shane's bare hand had sufficed to quiet him.

The silence of this vast land seemed absolute. In his soul Jones felt the stillness of this desolate Arizona to be a sinister thing; a thing of menace, dangerous and creeping, a thing that mocked and followed one about with saturnine leer. Only Shane seemed unaffected. Only the creak of saddle leather, the occasional jingle of spurs and the muffled plopping of the horses' hoofs disturbed the monstrous hush.

All this country appeared to be waiting, Jones thought bodingly. Mystery crouched upon its mountain crags; stark threat scowled hotly from its deserts. Even the vegetation was equipped with stinging spikes and there was a grim formidability about its animal life. It was a land whose paramount law was survival of the fittest— a hell where weaklings shriveled and died.

Though the hour was late they did not find Silver King completely dark. Three dives were open, throwing hurdles of yellow light across the dusty road. They filled the night around with confusion, noise and raucous laughter. As he listened to the brassy notes of a decrepit piano and a dance hall girl's high treble wail Jones thought more kindly of the desert's silence and would have welcomed it for a space.

Shane led the way to the largest establishment where they swung down and tethered their mounts to a spot Shane chose near the end of the hitching rail. Then, loosening his gun in its holster, Shane said quietly, "Let's go," and led the way through the swinging doors.

The place was far from crowded. Neither was it deserted. Several men bellied the crude plank bar that marked off its farther end. There were several gambling layouts being desultorily patronized and a tiny bit of cleared floor about the tin-panny piano where gen-tlemen might sling a wicked hoof with the percentage girls who draped their slinky forms about the room.

Jones, having noted the misspelled sign as they were entering, knew this dive for the Red Hoss Saloon of one R. Fogle, prop.

He kept his glance divided between Fogle's cus-tomers and Shane, alert and wary for his cue. Shane seemed perfectly at ease as he stood there squinting complacently through the smoke of his cigarette, thumbs hooked in his cartridge belt, his form in a hip-shot slouch.

No one seemed to be paying them any great attention, he thought, but watched suspiciously—none the less—three hombres who were standing with heads together whispering, halfway down the bar. One, a square-bodied, square-faced towhead with popping blue eyes and a cracklike mouth amid a maze of whiskers, seemed to be talking most of the time and he waved his hands emphatically to illustrate his argument.

Jones' lids closed down till only slits of his eyes were visible as he stared more closely at the trio. There was something wrong with that picture, he told himself. What it was he could not so easily define, but there was something. . . .

He looked at Shane. Shane appeared to pay the men no notice, yet as one of them abruptly left his companions and swung his steps in their direction, Jones saw Shane wheel slightly with a deep drag on his cigarette.

It was the square-faced towhead who approached. He stopped a few feet off and said to Shane, "Ain't yore name Shane?"

Jones saw a red-haired man with heavy lips edging toward them from behind the gambling tables and unostentatiously dropped his right hand to let it rest upon his gun as Shane said,

"Do I know you, friend? Your face don't seem uncommon familiar. Perhaps you've made a mistake," he added softly.

"Yo're Shane, ain't yuh?" the towhead persisted.

"What gives you that idea?"

"Why, yuh matches the desc—" he bit his words off short, cheeks darkening, popping eyes sinking dangerously inward. "Ne'mind. All I wanta know is are yuh the gent called S. G. Shane?"

The man's companions, and the red-head still edging closer, appeared to be listening with strained attention, as though something vital might hang upon Shane's acceptance of the name. Jones felt a cold chill of warning along his spine. His hand closed more firmly about the butt of his holstered gun as he waited for Shane's reply.

Shane's slow glance swept keenly over those others, and over the onlookers who had stopped all other business to watch the towhead and his companions as though fascinated. A chill seemed to have descended on the Red Hoss Saloon that was very different to its wonted atmosphere. Shane must have detected this for Jones observed the smoky hue of his eyes grow darker, dangerous. Tiny fires coalesced within their depths.

Shane seemed to maintain an attitude of aloof and suspended judgment.

"Are you Shane, or ain't yuh?" the towhead rasped with an oath.

The calm tranquillity of Sudden's glance was maddening; even Jones could feel the tightening tension which had almost reached the snapping point. The towhead's cheeks flamed red.

Shane said with leisured drawl, "Why, yes, my name is Shane, pardner. Were you aimin' to give me a reception—you and these other gents with the nervous feet?"

The towhead watched Shane with saturnine grin.

"Reception's right!" he jeered. "An' I'm figurin' to run it. I'm figurin' to run you outa town on a rail, with a nice coat of tar an' feathers, Mister Gunman Shane!"

"Really?" Shane chuckled.

"Yo're damn' right—really!"

"What for?" Shane asked, and "How did you get elected for the job?"

"I'm Marshal here," the towhead snarled, hand spreading claw-like above his holstered pistol. "You git outa this town pronto or you'll git put out plenty rough."

Shane's white teeth gleamed behind his parted lips. "I reckon I ain't never been put out of no place yet. An' I'm allowin' I don't expect I ever will. So you can get on with your tar-an'-featherin' an' your rail-ridin' any time you've a mind to. Go ahead, fella."

The towhead seemed a trifle taken aback by this unexpected situation. Jones saw his eyes flash hurriedly to where the red-head stood and turned his own glance in that direction just in time to catch the red-head's nod.

Shane's voice lashed out with a truculent snap, "Go on, hombre! Ain't no one settin' on your shirt-tail! Let loose your howlin' wolf!" And with the words, Jones saw Shane's gun snap out and stop tensely with its muzzle in the folds of the towhead's quivering stomach. The towhead's hands shot ceilingward with comical alacrity.

Shane grinned. "That's better," he drawled. "So you scorpions were figurin' to cold-deck Sudden Shane. My, my! Your audacity astounds me. Tell your friends, Whitey, to back up against the bar. They better have their paws up where I can look 'em over without

184

strainin' my eyes, too. I've got a itchy trigger-finger an' when my eyes start hurtin' I'm right apt to have a convulsion in that finger. That," his voice grew jeering, "would be awful bad for you."

Jones grinned as the towhead's friends began reluctantly retreating toward the bar. Shane certainly had a way with him, he felt. But Shane had ought to make those hombres part with their guns, he thought. First thing a—

"Lookout, boss!" he yelled frantically. *"This is it!"*

From the tail of his eyes Jones had seen the redhead's hand flash downward. Now it was coming up, gun-weighted, and there was a glint of triumphant satisfaction in the fellow's red-rimmed eyes.

Jones palmed his gun in a lightning motion even as Shane dropped below the other's shot. Came the rasp of steel on leather as Shane's long gun came out, while Shane with a roaring oath threw his body backward even as its muzzle cleared the holster, spat.

Belatedly the towhead's hand dived hipward. But it never reached his gun. Shane's shot took him in the shoulder, hurled him backward, smashed him against the bar.

Jones noted this subconsciously even as he slammed a shot at Fogle; missed, and fired again. Fogle staggered back beneath the bullet's shock but held his feet, striving valiantly to bring his gun to bear again. But in vain. Jones fired again and saw the red-head topple.

Then Shane's voice, over-riding the tumult of reverberating echoes that churned the narrow space:

"The door—*quick!*"

Even with the words Shane began backing toward it, the gun in his hand weaving from left to right, holding the snarling crowd momentarily in check. One man dared dart a hand to waist. Shane slammed in a shot from the hip that knocked him sprawling across a poker table, carrying it, cards, chips, white money and a bottle of rotgut to the floor in a splintering crash.

The hands of the white-faced, cowed but sullen crowd reached upward with renewed zest.

Jones had reached the door. "Out quick!" came Shane's command. "I'll follow."

Jones backed out, his gun too held level at the hip; backed out and turned to see if the way was clear.

All he saw was a livid burst of flame that split before his eyes. The smashing rip of lead hurled him back against the doors where with outspread arms he hung poised for a fleeting instant. Then the muscles of his body loosened, spilled him backward across the floor at the feet of Shane. He was dead before he struck.

Shane's lips parted in a savage snarl that was like the cry of some wounded animal. That was all; he did not curse. But a spinning leap took him through the doors with flaming gun. He grinned with ghastly mirthless-ness as his bullets drove Jones' killer to his knees in the dusty road. He laughed at the bloody sob in the man's clogged voice. Then he caught the pound of charging boots behind him.

With a slanchwise leap he scooped from the dust the killer's fallen gun and whirled, sliding his own emp-tied weapon back in leather, as the swinging doors bulged open to the headlong impact of the towhead's charging friends.

His lips curled back in a vicious snarl as he straightened to a crouch; eyes slitted, fiercely blazing. "So it's fight you want?" he lashed. "Well, *come an' get it!*"

With a cold fury almost unbelievable Shane drove his shots deliberately into that huddle of charging, cursing men. Gun thunder rose in huge crescendo, slamming heavily against the dark shadows of buildings across the street. The smashing rip of lead dropped the milling horde like quail.

Shouts, screams, curses intermingled in a tangled bedlam with the raucous bark of Colts. Through the red confusion some of the outlaws pistoled wildly. But their aim was mad, their trigger-fingers shaking. Shane's deadly aim demoralized their purpose. And suddenly, knowing their cause a lost one, those who could turned tail.

The thing was over as swiftly as it started. Against the yellow bar of lamplight streaming out beneath the doors, forms sprawled in crumpled limpness made grotesque, huddled blotches.

White-cheeked and sick from the terrible debacle Shane lurched blindly down the steps toward saddled horses, groaning as his clumsy fingers jammed fresh cartridges in his empty weapons.

Only vaguely was he aware of the disturbed ant-heap Silver King had now become. He hardly noticed the lights that were suddenly flaring in darkened windows, the half-clad men emerging hurriedly from false-fronted dwellings. His mind was filled with the image of Bless Jones—the lanky Britisher who never again would ride and laugh and curse and follow his lead on tortuous trails in dead of night. Jones, who had gone down fighting to the last.

CHAPTER EIGHTEEN

To the girl who rode with wrists tied behind her back and legs lashed by their ankles beneath her horse's belly alongside Jarson Lume through the brightening light of dawn, it seemed that Fate was a cruel and bitter thing; that life was hard and the world an empty laugh of cold indifference.

Nothing but a series of griefs and hardships, of struggles and forlorn hopes marked the backtrail through her short span of years; ahead loomed a seared and blistered desert of shattered dreams. For the first time in months her shoulders sagged. What was the use of going on living? What had life to offer her? she wondered.

She somberly studied Lume's broad back where he rode a few paces in the lead. Every line and curve of that black frock coat was hateful. Even the slant of his wide-brimmed, flat-crowned hat seemed to mock and jeer at her, seemed to sneer with cold complacency at her fate. He did not even look around; he knew that she would follow, that she dared not turn her horse aside. Worse—she was forced to admit that he was right.

To leave this trail they followed, tied like a steer for slaughter, must surely spell disaster for this was a wild and desolate country through which they traveled. A country of few and scattered ranches; a land where one might ride for hours without sighting a single moving creature.

No, she dared not try to elude him, not here. To do so here meant death of thirst, of exposure; a death so tortured she dared not contemplate it even. But surely, she reasoned listlessly, death of contact with the desert was better by far than the thing Lume held in store for her!

Lume had gloatingly told her not half an hour ago that Shane was on their trail. He had told her, grinning wickedly, that he had aroused a reception committee to greet Shane at Silver King—a committee whose business it was to see that he got no further. He had pointed out that since she now could hold no hope of getting away, she might as well behave.

She had heaped abuse upon him with scorn and loathing, vowing she'd have nothing to do with him were he the last man, even, on earth. But Lume had only grinned his taunting grin.

Sunrise came to light the world, to gild this desolate wilderness through which they rode with the rainbow colors of hope and promise. But Lize Corbin's lips twisted bitterly as she watched through haggard eyes. Life held no longer any promise worth redeeming, and as for hope—well, hope was dead.

"When we get to Globe," Lume's voice came chuckling back, "you'll have your final chance to get hitched up. You better make up your mind before we get there, too, 'cause I ain't figurin' to linger none. Not that there's any hurry now," he added quickly. "But I'm some anxious to get on to Bylas—I got a deal on there."

Lize Corbin held a scornful silence. Why give the

beast the satisfaction of an answer?

"Lucky the Indians are feelin' fat an' peaceful now," Lume continued. "It was along this trail the other side of Globe that that bunch of sneakin' redskins chopped the soldiers all to hell a short while back." He laughed with reminiscent glee. "I sold 'em some of the firewater that got 'em started. Figured it was a good way of keepin' attention away from Tortilla Flat."

Lize shuddered.

They rode a spell in silence. Then Lize thought she saw a way of getting under his skin as he was so constantly getting under hers. This talk of Indians was his idea of pleasantry. She believed she knew a way of taking that sneering grin from his mouth—for a time, at least.

"Y'u know," she said, as though thoughtfully, "y'u have been leavin' Stone Latham out of yo' figgerin'. He ain't goin' to like this business at all."

"What business?"

"This runnin' away with me. Stone Latham's a man to nurse a grudge an'—"

Lume's hateful laugh came floating back to interrupt her. "I reckon you're figurin' to tell me you an' him's been married," he jeered. "Don't waste your breath; I know all about it. No need for you to get all lathered up pinnin' any hopes on *him*."

"What do y'u mean?" Lize asked, a cold chill of premonition chasing the color from her cheeks. She had nothing but hate and loathing for Latham; but of the two she feared Jarson Lume the most. Jarson Lume who always got his way. "What do y'u mean about pinnin' any hopes on him?"

"He ain't in no position to be takin' up my trail right now," Lume's husky chuckle was sinister. "Him an' me has had a understandin'.""

"Understandin'?"

"Yeah. He ain't got no objections to you hitchin' up with me. Said he didn't give a damn who you hitched up with next. Now," his voice grew suave and soothing, "you ought to be right glad to marry a man as big as me. I'm one of the biggest men in this country. I'm goin' to be bigger, too. I'm figurin' to settle down an' quit my hell-bendin' ways. I want a home, a wife, an' kids. I want you—"

"What y'u want, y'u lyin' polecat, is the information yo' figgerin' Dry-Camp Corbin passed on to me after some of yo' bushwhackers give him a dose of lead-poi-sonin'!"

"Now see here," Lume growled, stopping his horse and hers, too, with a hand upon the check-strap. "I've had enough of your tantrums. An' I've had all I want of your damned insinuations. You better make up your mind to side with me; I'm figurin' on goin' places. Hell, nothin's too big for me to get, gal! I got property—rich property—all over this damn state. Look," he dropped his voice confidentially, "I got my eye on the gov-ernor's seat right now."

"I don't give a durn if yo' got yo' eye on the Presi-dent's seat; y'u ain't goin' to get me! Why," Lize cried with unutterable scorn, "I'd kill myself first!"

Lume chuckled. "Yeah? Well, I'll see that you don't get no chance, then. What you figurin' to save yourself

191

for, gal? Not Latham, sure? An' Shane is goin' to get himself rubbed out real quick—may be rubbed out now, I shouldn't wonder. Don't be a fool. I can give you anything you want; all the things you never had—good clothes, jewelry, position. Cripes, you stick with me, Lize, an' I'll take you places."

"Yeah, I bet y'u will." Her voice was drily sarcastic, "Jail, prob'ly, or the owlhoot trail!"

Lume snorted "There ain't no man in the country big enough to shove Jarson Lume in a jail! Act your age, gal. I got this country sewed up. I can control the courts, I'm bossin' the minin' camps where most of the dinero is; I own some of the biggest ranches an' I've got a interest in them I don't own outright. What the hell more could you ask?"

"All that is so, I reckon," Lize said wearily. "But I'm not wantin' y'u, an' yo' not gettin' me. So make up yo' mind to it."

"I ain't, eh?" Lume's husky tones turned ugly. "We'll see about that!"

With a swift cruel yank he jerked her toward him; one sinewy arm about her shoulders effectually preventing her from getting free of him. Bound as she was at wrist and ankles her struggles were so futile as to draw a mocking grin to Lume's bloodless, clean-shaven face. "Spirit," he purred, "is what I like in my string."

Lize's cheeks were alabaster white; her lips colorless lines of loathing as Lume, with a sudden oath, bent her back across his left forearm. Then his face thrust close to hers. "There's no time like the present," he snarled, "for learnin' you who's the boss!"

He cupped a hand about her left breast and burned her face with his kisses. He left her white and breathless and with pounding heart. Her eyes held the flame of murder.

He laughed as he let her go and his handsome, bloodless face held satisfaction. "By Gawd, but you're a beauty, gal!" His lewd glance played across the litheness of her body. "You've got what it takes!"

The lure of her seemed to rock him. He half leaned forward again as though to learn if her charms would improve upon acquaintance. But somehow she maneuvered her horse aside and saw him straighten with a chuckle.

"No more just now, eh? Well, you've earned your way, for the moment. But you're mine, an' don't forget it! I've put my brand on you, gal! You belong to Jarson Lume!"

Two hours had passed since Sudden Shane had left the noisy turbulence of Silver King behind. It was light now, and although he had closely scanned his backtrail many times since dawn he had seen no sign of pursuit. He looked again, half turning in his saddle. But the rugged terrain behind loomed empty and desolate as ever. With a breath of relief he swung his eyes to the front, to the hoofprints of the pair of horses he had followed since the vanishing of darkness had permitted him to scan the trail.

One, he could see by the sign, was a paddler, and faster than its companion. The other was a "coon-footed" bronc of low pasterns. Neither was hurrying now, and Shane guessed that Lume had slowed the pace to conserve their endurance.

"Must be figurin' to cover a heap of territory," Shane opined. "I shouldn't wonder but what Jarson's aimin' to cut his stick."

His lips pressed tightly together at the thought, and the muscles bunched along his jaw. "Figurin' to take Lize Corbin clear out of the country."

The horse on which Shane had departed from Silver King was a good one. And lucky that it was, he reflected grimly, for there were not apt to be many places on the trail Lume was traveling where re-mounts could be secured. Lume was deliberately avoiding all common lanes of travel, sticking to the rough country, the desert wastes and rock-choked canyons where he would not be apt to encounter other riders who might get curious about the girl.

Shane's horse was a short-coupled blue roan, probably weighing a good eleven hundred pounds; an animal promising a deal more endurance than speed, but one that, properly handled, could cover ground for days. And Shane was of the opinion that the chase might well last that long unless some unforeseen circumstance intervened.

This horse of his, he reasoned, had likely belonged to one of those gunfighters he and Jones had encountered in the saloon of the Red Hoss. The saddle was ornately carved and heavily embossed with silver; a kak of the rim-fire type. A rifle scabbard was slung at an approximately horizontal position on the near side of the horse, passing between the two leaves of the stirrup-leather. A good repeater lay inside it, butt forward. He had examined it and found it fully loaded, and had discovered that there were more shells for it in one of the leathern pouches slung from the saddle horn.

He was well armed, having besides the rifle, that extra pistol he had snatched from the dust where Jones' killer had fallen. The loops of his belt had provided, however, barely sufficient cartridges to fill them. Should he shoot these out he would have to discard the belt guns and take to the rifle, a more awkward weapon in the event of close-range work.

The mutations of Shane's wandering thoughts turned his mind again to Lize. Where was she? he wondered, and was she safe? Reason and logic told him that she must be safe so far, at any rate, for Lume's headlong flight could spare the man scant time for dalliance. But should Lume hole up. . . .

Shane dared not contemplate the possibilities of such an event.

In the chaparral stretches, in the blistering sand, in the glassy white of the midday sky he could see Lisabet's vision clearly—as clear and graphic, almost, as though she were there before him. He was startled, nevertheless, when looking toward the shimmering horizon he saw, in the near distance, a patch of rocky trail with two riders astride of motionless horses upon it. One rider was a woman—he could tell by the tawny hair that hung below her hat. He could tell it by her face which abruptly was turned in his direction; the face of Lize! Her wrists were lashed together behind her back and her ankles tied beneath her horse's belly. The other rider was the man in a flat-crowned hat and a black frock coat whom Shane had no difficulty in recognizing as Lume.

Shane was so startled he involuntarily checked the blue roan's forward progress and sat there motionless, intent upon the drama being unreeled on the rocky trail. He saw Lume sway toward Lize and pull her toward him with a savage arm about her shoulders; saw Lume bend her back across that arm and cover her upturned face with kisses.

Shane's eyes were narrowed, blazing slits when Lume released the girl and sat regarding her with gloating grin. Shane's lips were white as his cheeks and a vein throbbed wildly on his forehead; his big fists were tensely bunched.

With a sense of nausea he saw Lume urge his horse in close to the girl's once more as though to renew his assaults while she struggled futilely against her bonds. Shane swore bitterly and raked the roan's flanks with reddening spurs. Yet as the horse lunged forward the riders, the rocky trail and all shivered, cracked and dissolved and naught remained where these things had been but sandy waste ashimmer with waves of heat.

A mirage!

But realization of the fact did not cause Shane to slow his mount's pace appreciably. Somewhere the scene he had just been witness to was happening! Shane dared not linger here nor longer conserve the blue roan's strength. Lize Corbin's reputation was at stake—her life, perhaps!

That her reputation already brought sneers to the

faces of righteous persons made no difference to Shane. *He* believed in Lize; believed her to be pure and sweet and good. His faith in her was above the evil tongue of scandal; whatever she had done, he thought, there must in her mind have been the best of reasons for her acts.

So it was that he drove the blue roan forward now, one eye alert upon the trail, the other keen for possible ambush. He had no means of knowing how far away the tableau he'd watched might be. But he meant to get there just as soon as this horse, by the grace of God and his own sharp flashing spurs, could cover the distance.

Forward, ever forward, they went plunging into the rush and slap of the searing wind that was like a draught from Hell's furnace. A half hour slid by with only the whistling wind, the creak of leather and pounding hoofs to tell that they were not within a vacuum. Shane might have thought they rode a treadmill but for the dizzy blur of chaparral, rocks, stunted oak and pig-locust reeling constantly by.

Then abruptly Shane regained control of his emotions and checked the ruinous pace of the gallant horse between his knees. This animal's strength must be preserved. One final burst of speed, or the hardy ground-eating endurance for which this horse was gaited, might finally spell the difference between shame and virtue, or between life and death, to the girl he loved.

They rode at times across timbered ridges where the wind-whipped tracery of clacking branches provided a screening lattice against the burning rays of the brassy sky.

At other times they rode through flat bottoms where

the vegetation was rank and stringy, and the sun beat down with unleashed venom that blistered all it touched.

Occasionally Shane would halt the blue roan's progress long enough to get down and closely study the tracks left by the horse of Lume and Lize. He stopped now for that purpose and, as he squatted there on his bootheels beside the shaley trail, a slow sardonic grin pulled at his lips. He was getting close; these tracks showed sudden hurry, proving that somehow Lume had sighted him and knew his Nemesis was drawing near.

Shane climbed back into the saddle with renewed confidence and hope. He now most definitely had Jarson Lume on the run; the man's actions, as shown by the hoofprints, proved it!

"He'd better slope!" Shane muttered grimly. "'Cause I'm allowin' when I catch up with him, the reckonin' he's been pilin' up these last weeks since I been in this country is goin' to be settled plumb permanent."

But if Jarson Lume had seen him and was, indeed, attempting flight through fear and desperation, he was putting his knowledge of the country to good use. The long afternoon wore slowly by and yet, when evening came, Shane still had failed to sight him. His only consolation was the reflection that Lume would not dare tarry to further his designs on Lize until a more propitious time. And this so-galling postponement of Shane's desire for vengeance but whetted his already feverish lust for blood.

CHAPTER NINETEEN

I T was dusk when Sudden Shane, tight of lip and grim of eye, rode into the copper town of Globe. Lights were beginning to come on in its houses, flinging slender lances, broad bars and glowing pools of golden radiance across the shadowed dirt of its broad main street.

Shane, after his long ride and weary hours in the saddle, was feeling pretty ganted as he swung stiffly from the blue roan before the hitch rack fronting the Copper City Grub Emporium and, tying the roan loosely to the rail, went inside cuffing the alkali grit from his clothing.

The restaurant was practically deserted at this hour. Shane saw no one at the counter but a whiskered old miner who lolled on his elbows above his emptied plate. The light in his faded eyes showed Shane his mind was far away; perhaps with the folks who, when setting out to make his fortune years agone, he'd left behind.

Shane took a stool at the counter's other end, from which position he could watch the door and any passers along the walk outside, who would be illuminated by the light streaming from the Emporium.

While his supper was being cooked in a back room Shane sat moody with his restless thoughts. Though he realized he must be pressing close to Lume, he felt anxious none the less about Lize Corbin. He could imagine well the nightmare this experience must be proving to her. Conjecture along these unpleasant lines brought out cold sweat upon his forehead.

When his food was placed before him he ate hurriedly, washing it down with cups of scalding coffee. He paid no attention to the plump and handsome waitress who was palpably willing to flirt. Indeed, he seemed not to even sense her presence.

His thoughts were still with Lize and his eyes, for the most part, remained focused on the door. He did not anticipate sighting any acquaintance here, but the turmoil of his border years had taught him caution, the value of being ever on his guard against surprise. Scarce wonder then that the waitress' many attentions went for naught.

As he ate he listened to the occasional snatches of conversation which drifted in from the night outside. The plank sidewalk rumbled hollowly to the oft uneven tread of booted feet as the citizens of Globe, their suppers eaten and their after-supper chores completed, set out to spend their loose change in such resorts as catered to their tastes. Lucky, carefree hombres. . . .

And then suddenly Shane's lean wiry form went tense. His cheeks went gray beneath their bronze as his eyes narrowed intently on the broad, black-frocked back of a tall man passing the door.

In an instant he was off his stool. Slipping a handful of change on the counter, he cat-footed swiftly to the door, passed through and onto the busy walk outside.

By the lights of stores and other business places he could see the tall man threading his way through the townsmen up ahead. He followed grimly, his narrowed eyes never leaving that black-frocked back.

So intent was he upon that man ahead that he jostled a red-shirted miner unintentionally off the walk. The fellow swore and Shane, never taking his glance from his quarry, apologized—but kept on moving.

A heavy hand caught him by the shoulder, whirled him round with a lurid oath. "Push me into that dust, will ye? By Gawd, I'll teach ye ter watch where ye're goin'!"

"No offense, pardner," Shane grinned, and would have started on. But the miner would not have it so; too much drink had made him ugly. He swung a haymaker at Shane's jaw which only missed by inches.

Shane swore and brought an angry right fist up from his bootstraps. It took the Cousin Jack glancingly upon his Adam's apple and thudded to a jarring stop beneath his stubbled chin. Without a sound of remonstrance the miner went over backwards, struck heavily on the walk. A flashing glance of Shane's keen eyes showed him other miners crowding up.

Shane squared off impatiently. "Listen, hombres; that gent got bumped off this walk by mistake. I was lookin' at someone else an' didn't see him. I apologized but he got tough."

"Aah, y'u damn' punchers think y'u own the world!" sneered another red-shirted fellow. "C'mon, boys, let's show this hard case what we do to leather-whackers in Globe! One of y'u git a rail! We'll fix 'im!"

Seeing that these men were not only ugly but determined to start a fracas, Shane knew from experience that he must take the offensive instantly. A man of action, no sooner had the thought flashed through his mind than he was wading in, caring not one whit what his lashing fists contacted so long as they struck home. He sent men reeling right and left before his furious onslaught. But he did not get clear. Others sprang to combat and he found himself hemmed in.

Striking, slugging, kicking, pounding, Shane swayed the sweating miners back and forth, bruising, maiming, cursing. This delay was making him frantic, for the man he'd been following was Lume!

The miners felt the turbulence of his emotions; his strength and endurance were those of a madman and the speed of his smashing fists incredible. One by one he bowled them down, or sent them staggering back into the gloomy shadows beyond reach of the lights where they gladly deserted the battle which had proved to be much hotter than they'd bargained for!

At last Shane found himself alone; alone, that is, save for a number of groaning ex-combatants scattered prostrate or on hands and knees about him on the plank walk and in the dust of the street.

But Lume, if Lume it had been, had vanished.

With a bitter oath Shane struck off down the walk with angry strides, glancing hurriedly into each place of business as he passed. With each progressive yard his anger grew until a raging passion was visible in his usually complacent gaze, and his mouth was a tight straight line.

Then, just as he was about to think that once again Lume had made good his escape, Lume came out of a cafe with several packages under one arm and without a glance to right or left continued down the street.

Cautiously, striding along behind a pair of conversing punchers, Shane followed, determined this time to trace the slippery Jarson to his lair.

Being careful that the punchers unconsciously screened him from Lume's vision, should Lume chance to glance around, each time he reached a lighted area, Shane followed his quarry to the Copper House, a dingy hotel on a side street where shadows were more than plentiful.

Waiting until Lume had passed within, Shane moved casually to the porch where a group of hard-faced loafers sat smoking in chairs tilted back against the wall. As casually, then, he strolled inside as Lume's boots disappeared up a staircase at the rear of the littered lobby.

Shane thoughtfully regarded the sallow-faced clerk behind the desk in a railed-off portion near the stairs while he rolled himself a smoke. The man's eyes slid about uneasily under Shane's steady regard.

A preacher clad in rusty black came in and stopped beside the desk. Shane caught the words distinctly as the sky-pilot asked:

"Can you tell me, brother, if Mr. Judson is in his room?"

The clerk regarded the sky-pilot suspiciously. But at last said, "Yeah—room ten."

The preacher thanked him and started up the stairs. Shane followed. The preacher paused before Number 10 and knocked. In a few moments Shane heard

Lume's voice call:

"Who's there?"

The preacher said, "The Reverend Wilkes."

Shane flattened himself against the wall as the door swung open long enough to admit Mr. Wilkes and then swung sharply shut behind him.

Shane waited, devil's temper stirring behind the smoky gray of his eyes.

Abruptly he heard the rise of angry voices from beyond the door. In three long strides he was outside it, crouching, one hand grasping the knob. Softly he turned it and, as he had suspected, found the door locked.

Then he heard Lize scream, *"I won't! Y'u'll never make me!"* And the preacher's quavery voice raised in protest.

Shane waited for no more but hurled himself against the door, fury rioting in his veins, but one coherent thought thrusting through the red madness in his brain. It was much more than a thought; it was a gripping white-hot desire—he must reach and destroy Lume instantly!

The door gave way with a rending, splintered crash and the momentum of his blow sent Shane lurching on within, his blazing eyes taking in the scene in one swift stabbing glance.

Lume was on the aggressive; his face was hideous and awful in its savage passion as he grabbed for Lize—and missed. Both whirled as the door crashed down. The preacher's face was deathly white. . . .

Jarson Lume cursed viciously, terribly as he glared.

Shane's lips were parted tautly over his hard white gleaming teeth; his rage was more awful than Lume's in the chill quiet of its intensity. His gray eyes, like smoking sage, alive with the cold warning of imminent violent action rode heavily across Lume's snarling features.

Lize Corbin's cheeks were deathly white, her lips entirely devoid of color.

The preacher like a statue stood, face gray, alarmed and fearful, his diminutive body taut. The room's temperature seemed to have dropped to zero, yet his forehead was steeped in sweat.

Shane's voice crossed the silence in a cold, wicked drawl:

"Lume, you've reached the end of your rope."

The atmosphere was aching while for two seconds there was silence. Lume broke it with a ripped-out curse and sent his right hand streaking inside his coat.

His gun glinted in the light, spat flame. But terror, or perhaps the passion that rocked him, shook his aim. The angry whine of his lead hemmed Shane; he could hear the bullets splintering the wall behind him. Then his gun was out. It barked shortly from his hip—just once. A grin parted his lips vindictively when Jarson Lume clutched his chest and crumpled backward across a table that went down beneath his weight.

Shane sheathed his gun and, leaping forward, caught Lize as she would have fallen in her reaction from the strain. Her arms closed round his neck convulsively and she hid a tear-wet face against his breast while great sobs shook her body.

The parson came out of his palsied trance and started for the door. But—

"Wait," Shane said, and stopped him with a foot still tautly raised in air. Shane laughed at his embarrassment and the look of ludicrous panic on his face. "I'm allowin'," Shane added, "we're goin' to have a use for you directly. It'll oblige me mighty much if you'd just stick around a spell."

Pulling free of his protecting arm Lize brushed the tears from her starry eyes. "I—I— We can't!" she muttered dully. "It wouldn't be right. Stone Latham knew Dad passed me on the secret of his discovery. The location of his strike, I mean. He made love to me—I thought it was love. I—I— We're married," she finished miserably. "No one knew it . . . that's how the talk got started. He—he was seen leaven' my place before daylight one mornin'. But we were married proper!" she added defiantly, looking at the parson.

"No one could doubt it, Lize," Shane told her gravely. "You are too fine, ma'am, for anythin' else. But you're not married to him any more. Stone Latham's dead— Lume pistoled him in Silver King. An' it don't make a shuck's worth of diff'rence to me whether Dry-Camp Corbin found gold or not—"

"But he *did!*" Lize interrupted excitedly. "He—"

"Makes no diff'rence. I got plenty dinero for both of us, an' a durn good ranch in Texas besides. Lize, there's nothin' more to hold me in this country but you. Obe Struthers, now Lume is finished, will get his mine back an' everythin' will be ironed out smooth as a whistle.

"Lize," Shane's voice grew soft with longing, "tomorrow's a new day. An' it's almost here." He flashed a significant look at the staring parson. "What say we start it right?"

Center Point Publishing
600 Brooks Road ● PO Box 1
Thorndike ME 04986-0001 USA

(207) 568-3717

US & Canada:
1 800 929-9108